D0375226

STOLEN KISSES

Sally Falcon

A KISMET™ Romance

METEOR PUBLISHING CORPORATION
Bensalem, Pennsylvania

To Lucy Robinson, Judy Craig, & Helen Barry, my fellow script committee members for the 1992 Quapaw Tours

Special acknowledgement to:

All the homeowners and hundreds of volunteers who have made the tours possible for thirty years.

SALLY FALCON

Sally lives in Arkansas and works full-time as a librarian when not writing. She enjoys traveling and likes to incorporate real settings in her books from the eight states she has lived in over the years. She also writes Regency romances as Sarah Eagle.

Other books by Sally Falcon:

No. 3 *SOUTHERN HOSPITALITY*
No. 30 *REMEMBER THE NIGHT*
No. 55 *A FOREVER MAN*

ONE

"Rub my ears, and I'd follow you anywhere, sugar."

The smooth masculine drawl homed in on the base of Jessie DeLord's spine, then sidled upward to come to rest between her shoulder blades. Without any outward sign of the sudden lack of oxygen to her brain, she blinked dispassionately at the six-foot rabbit that had suddenly materialized next to her. He was a strange apparition, even at a costume party celebrating Harry Houdini's birthday.

"Hi, darlin', I'd sure like to be your bunny for the rest of the night," he continued, his inflection making it clear he'd like to spend their time together in a horizontal position.

"I beg your pardon?" she managed in a breathless voice that was supposed to have been haughty and highly offended. Why had she allowed Gina to talk her into wearing this ridiculous abbreviated magician's-assistant costume to the Bushes' party? She wasn't the type for black fish-net stockings and scarlet satin trimmed in black lace ruffles.

"Darlin', you aren't goin' ta break ole Trevor's heart

so soon? You wound me.'' He punctuated the declaration by clasping his hand over his heart, his drawl more exaggerated with each syllable. A thoroughly masculine inspection, beginning at her feet and sweeping upward over the sixty-six inches of her paralyzed frame, counteracted his crestfallen expression. Jessie's gaze was drawn inexorably to a well-toned example of the Southern male chest, since he was wearing only a white vest on his upper torso.

"Aren't you late for a very important date?" The words tripped out before she could stop herself. He didn't need any encouragement, so she redoubled her effort without regard to the manners her mother had drilled into her throughout her childhood. "Who *are* you?"

"I'm Trevor." A slanted smile accompanied the singular announcement. To preserve her sanity she raised her eyes to the pair of three-foot pink-and-white ears that flopped in the air above his thick brown hair. "I want to take you away from all this nonsense."

She closed her eyes, counting to twenty for good measure. Maybe she was hallucinating and he would be gone when she opened her eyes again. Daring to raise one eyelid, she discovered that he was still there, his head cocked slightly to one side as he waited patiently for her to respond. With a sigh of resignation, she opened both eyes in complete empathy with Alice's confusing experience with her own white rabbit.

"Did Gina Caryle put you up to this?" There had to be a reason he was hitting on her, probably one of her devious best friend and business partner's machinations; this usually didn't happen to Jessie. Normally she was buttonholed by someone's grandfather or elderly uncle, not a predatory male who could have his choice of any available, or unavailable, woman in the room. Not that she would want anything to do with that type of male.

Since he seemed to be a lunatic, maybe her luck was running true to form.

"Sorry, I don't know her, but she couldn't be as gorgeous as you. Now, about later tonight. I promise to show you all the best places in Wonderland," he stated firmly, moving closer to occupy her personal space. The warmth of his body and an alluring whiff of British Sterling cologne only added to her bemused state of mind.

"Here's your mineral water, Jessica. Do you believe the crush of people at this party?" Connor MacMurray asked, seeming to have appeared from nowhere. He gave the man standing next to her only a cursory look, though Trevor's genial grin had disappeared.

"I was just beginning to wonder if you'd disappeared, Connor," Jessie murmured in relief, giving her date a slight smile. It was the most she'd said to him since he arrived on her doorstep; they'd discussed the weather then. She had met him only recently, when Abby Bush had introduced them during an intermission at the Rep two weeks earlier, and now she was finding this first date heavy going. The attorney had seemed to step off her prime candidate's list for the ideal husband—late thirties, an established job, responsible demeanor, and no visible faults. Characteristics that probably weren't shared by a rabbit named Trevor, despite his conversational talents.

"There was a mob of people around the bar, which Gary set up in the kitchen," Connor continued, seeming impervious to Trevor's now glowering presence. "People always congregate in the kitchen, so why put the bar in there? Not good planning."

Jessie took the glass he held out, her smile fixed in place. If Connor continued to complain, she didn't think she was going to get Trevor to go away without saying something outrageous. Though she'd only known the amorous rabbit a few minutes, she was sure he wasn't intimidated by many situations or people. Fortunately he seemed content with the awkward silence that descended among the three of them.

A sharp whistle cut through the noisy chatter of the crowd, and Jessie purposefully centered her attention on her hostess at the far end of the crowded game room. Becoming engrossed in the evening's entertainment was just the diversion she needed.

So how can you consider Connor a potential husband if you can't even talk to him? The taunting voice in her head sounded suspiciously like Gina's. Surreptitiously she studied the two men. Both were about six feet tall, a comfortable six inches taller than she. While Trevor's whipcord leanness looked natural in the white chinos and vest, Connor's stocky figure resembled a taxidermist's dream in his rented tux. She knew Connor was her own age, but she wasn't sure which side of thirty-five to place Trevor. There was a boyish air to his ear-bedecked brown hair as well as the mischievous twinkle in his almond-shaped brown eyes; Connor was the epitome of conservatism from his closely cropped blond hair to his serviceable wing tips. Trevor's slightly crooked nose gave him the ideal look for a Bad-Boys-'R'-Us poster next to Connor's impersonation of a Young Republican recruiter.

Unconsciously sighing in regret, Jessie wondered just how long it would take her to find the ideal husband and, more important, a potential father candidate. At thirty-eight, she knew that the last few grains of sand were slipping through the maternity hourglass. She was looking for the solid conservative type, because she knew from years of experience that charming, flirtatious men simply were not dependable.

"Can I have y'all's attention? *Pull-leeze!*" At Abby Bush's exasperated plea from her perch on a makeshift platform, Jessie redoubled her efforts to focus her attention. Her hostess flapped her black silk cape to capture the rest of her guests' wandering attention. "The food is just about ready, so it's show time."

A good-natured groan went up from the crowd, which didn't deter her. "You know the rules: Those that wants ta eat has ta perform." The expected announcement was met by catcalls and a few Bronx cheers. "Come on, y'all, magic tricks are much easier than last year for the Mozart birthday bash. Nobody has to murder a minuet this time." The crowd cheered. "Now, if I can just find my master of ceremonies, we'll get started."

"I guess that's my cue," Trevor announced, unfortunately bringing Jessie's awareness back to him.

"You're the master of ceremonies?" She grasped at anything to ignore the sexy glint in his eyes, one that seemed to say they shared an illicit secret. Without being aware of it, she moved closer to Connor.

"Sure thing, darlin'. That way I don't have to perform any magic tricks," he replied easily, seeming impervious to her attempt to look indifferent. "Once I do my duty, we can get back to our earlier conversation."

Giving her a broad wink, he sauntered away to make his presence known to his hostess. The other guests greeted his approach with amiable contempt, and his complacent handling of each insult fascinated Jessie against her will.

"Jessica, who was *that?*"

Connor's outraged question saved her from her own traitorous thoughts about the rabbit tail fixed tantalizingly to the seat of Trevor's chinos. Shaking her head to clear the last remnant of the white rabbit's smile from her subconscious, Jess turned her attention to her companion. *This is the man you're spending the evening with, Jessica Marie,* she told herself sternly for good measure. *You have an important goal, and you can't achieve it if you're so easily distracted.* With a last look over her shoulder at the master of ceremonies' smiling face, she took a deep breath and resolutely said, "So, Connor, tell me about your current caseload."

Two hours later, Jessie tried to ignore the throbbing pain in her left temple.

"Can you believe the woman actually took an ax to the man's Mercedes? I've handled some tricky property settlements before, but this was downright incredible." Connor was now into the details of his seventh divorce case. Jessie regretted that she'd mentioned his work, even if it was standard dating etiquette. The man not only sided with every male client, he thought all his clients were fools to be married in the first place.

"Connor—"

"She said if she couldn't have the car, then no one was—"

"Connor!" She almost smiled in satisfaction at the startled look on his face at her slightly shrill tone. Apparently Connor MacMurray was not accustomed to being interrupted. "Connor, I've developed a dreadful headache. Would you mind taking me home now?"

"Yes, I can see how all this noise would bring one on," he agreed with a superior look at the boisterous people around them, oblivious to the fact that he was the cause of her migraine. "I'll get our coats and see if I can find our host in this madhouse."

Jessie breathed a sigh of relief, noticing that her headache began to diminish immediately. Stepping back near the wall, she was glad for the potted fig tree next to her that shielded her from the other guests. Unlike Connor, she had enjoyed the rowdy crowd, but she needed a few minutes to herself. She closed her eyes and tipped back her head to rest against the cool surface behind her. How was she quickly going to dismiss Connor and his oversized ego once they arrived at her house?

"Logan, are you sure you haven't seen her? She's about five-six, has black hair and the face of a princess?"

Jessie didn't have to open her eyes to know *that* voice, but she did. Turning her head slightly to one side, she held her breath at the sight of white ears peeking through the leaves of the fig tree. Although Trevor had his back to her, his companion was staring right at her. His angular face gave no sign of recognition.

"Trevor, that describes about half the women in the room," the man stated evenly as he watched Jessie start to back away shaking her head from side to side.

"She's in a cute little red outfit and has legs that go on forever. Does that help?"

"Well, that narrows it down to one or two, including that woman you grabbed from behind a few minutes ago and whose husband almost decked you," his friend responded just as Jessie turned away and hurried in the opposite direction.

She didn't bother to look back, keeping her gaze trained directly in front of her. Though she had seen Trevor several times during the evening, this was the first time he hadn't been across the room with a woman practically attached to his hip. She was surprised Button Mainwairing had let the precocious rabbit out of her snare. He was undoubtedly the rapacious woman's type; Button had already worked her way through two husbands and, according to the latest rumor, was almost through with number three. She, however, had had some competition for the wily rabbit's attention from an attractive brunette in a turquoise jumpsuit. Not that Trevor's conquests were any of Jessie's business.

"Jessie, there you are. I've been searching all over for you."

She relaxed when she recognized the voice of her hostess. "Abby, I was just looking for you to say goodnight," she exclaimed, smiling at the petite blonde. "I had a terrific time."

"Then why are you leaving so soon? I promise there won't be any more magic tricks," Abby added quickly, a perpetual twinkle of amusement in her eyes. Her optimistic attitude and forthright nature ensured that Abby had a large circle of friends.

"That was fun, but I have a full day tomorrow. Gina and I have a major presentation for T. L. Planchet coming up," she explained, not wanting Abby to know she thought Connor was a blockhead. "This is Aesthetics, Ltd.'s big break into the corporate sector. Quite a step up from redecorating a three-room real estate office."

"Then don't rush off before I introduce you to—"

"I've been looking everywhere for you," two male voices broke in simultaneously. Both Jessie and Abby looked in confusion from the frowning rabbit to the scowling man at his side. Jessie wanted to sink through the floor as her headache returned full force. She'd almost made a clean getaway.

"Connor, there you are! I was just saying good-night to Abby while you were getting our coats," Jessie exclaimed, letting the words tumble over one another. She kept her eyes trained on her date as she continued to babble. "I really hate to leave, but I have so much work piled up that I'll have to work all weekend just to catch up. Abby, it was truly a lovely party. I'll call you soon about lunch, and we can catch up on all the news then. This party was such a fun idea—"

Only a step away from her date's side, she was sure she was going to succeed in ignoring Trevor. Unfortunately, he had other ideas about her sudden departure.

His hand closed on her upper arm as he murmured, "Jessie, darlin', it was great seeing you again."

The warm touch of his palm against her bare skin seemed to paralyze every muscle in her legs. She managed to turn halfway toward him to demand that he let go of her at once. But the protest was smothered against the surprising touch of his lips. She lost all awareness of time and place. Everything but the man holding her disappeared from sight. As the room seemed to spin out of control, she clutched at Trevor's bare shoulders to keep her balance. The heat suffusing her body only intensified as his hand moved smoothly down her spine.

Then it was over. She blinked in confusion, wondering if they'd been locked in an embrace for a minute or a half hour. Gradually she began to regain her equilibrium. First she was able to focus her vision on the grinning man in front of her, then her hearing started to come back. As she recognized the sputtering noises coming from Connor, Trevor gave her a two-fingered salute and walked away without saying a word.

"Jessica, who was that jackass?"

She heard Connor's outraged question from a great distance, wanting foolishly to say, "That was a rabbit." She'd known Trevor was a dangerous nuisance the moment she looked into his sleepy brown eyes, but she certainly never expected anything as volatile as *that*. Shaking her head to clear the last remnant of the sensual haze her white rabbit left in his wake, she shoved her arms into the coat that Connor was still holding. With an absent nod to her hostess she headed for the door, not bothering to see if her date was following her.

"Do you mind telling me why you're accosting women at my party?"

Trevor slowly lowered the bottle of beer he'd been

about to drink from for the third time in the last two minutes. Dispassionately he noted his hand wasn't quite steady. His hostess was slightly miffed, he decided as he leaned his right hip against the kitchen counter, still trying to shake off the shock waves set off by kissing Jessie. What had started out as a teasing salute had quickly turned into something he didn't want to analyze too closely. How was he going to explain it to the aggravated woman in front of him?

"Sorry, Abby, but that stuffed-shirt boyfriend of hers got on my nerves earlier," he stated for lack of any logical explanation. Normally he had impeccable manners. "It was just one of those devilish impulses."

"One of these days those impulses are going to get you into serious trouble," she returned heatedly, her fists still planted on her hips. "Connor may not be the ideal date for Jessie, but she's too nice for a smooth-talking stud like you."

"Smooth-talking stud?" He couldn't resist laughing at her exaggerated description. Abby was always trying to find the right partners for her friends, redoubling her efforts since her own marriage. The only two people who had escaped her clutches were his sister, who was Abby's boss, and himself. She swore she wasn't going to inflict instant heartache on any of her friends by introducing them to him.

"I'll have to call Jessie tomorrow and apologize for one of my guests pawing her," Abby continued, giving him another stern look. "Of course, she may not be speaking to me either, since I introduced her to Connor a few weeks ago."

So the blockhead isn't a permanent fixture in Jessie's life. Trevor almost smiled at the thought but rigidly kept his expression properly chastened for Abby's benefit. He didn't want her to know that his interest in Jessie was any deeper than playing a joke on her escort. "I suppose I should be the one to apologize, since I was the transgressor,'' he said innocently and accompanied the statement with his best I'm-outrageous-but-harmless smile.

''You stay away from Jessica DeLord,'' she warned with a pointed finger for good measure.

Bingo! The name *DeLord* suited her regal stance, he decided. She had looked very royal when he first approached her after admiring her from across the room for a half hour. The cascade of inky black curls that surrounded her flawless oval face, however, tempted a man to bury his fingers in the silky tresses. In his haste, he'd been clumsy, but he'd seen the momentary look of surprise in her gorgeous blue eyes before her remote mask slipped into place. The sound of her husky Lauren Bacall voice still sounded in his subconscious. A whisky-smooth voice, cornflower-blue eyes, delicate features, and legs that went on forever—no man could resist the lure.

''Trevor Planchet, have you heard one word I've said to you?''

The sound of Abby's voice broke into his lecherous daydreams. He blinked to bring her back into focus. ''Now, Abby, it was just a little joke, that's all.''

''Have you been propositioning my wife again?'' Gary Bush slipped his arm around his wife's shoulder, stroking his beard in a menacing manner. ''Find your own woman, Planchet.''

''I'm trying, I'm trying,'' he protested, raising his hands in the air in a show of total surrender. ''She's picking on me again.''

''Probably no more than you deserve after that kiss I saw you plant on Jessie DeLord earlier,'' Gary returned with an affable grin. ''She's too nice for the likes of you.''

''It's a conspiracy. All I did was kiss the woman

because her escort was behaving like a horse's ass," he prevaricated. He didn't think mentioning that she had the most kissable mouth he'd ever seen would be very politic at the moment.

"I told Abby that she shouldn't inflict ol' Connor on anyone she liked, but she just wouldn't listen," her husband stated, only to be rewarded with a sharp elbow in the ribs.

"He came up to you at the Rep while we were talking during intermission." She gave her husband an aggrieved look as she countered his accusation. "You didn't bother to tell me until later that he was the biggest bore in Arkansas. Jessie is one of the nicest women I know, so I wouldn't intentionally pair her up with a dud. Which is why I was warning off the kissing bandit here."

"I think I liked being a stud better," Trevor announced, wondering how he was going to get more information out of his overprotective hostess. Why did Jessie have to be a close friend of hers?

"Well, she wouldn't have time for you anyway. She's much too busy getting her design firm established," Abby announced as if that settled the matter once and for all.

Trevor answered her triumphant smile with one of his own. If the conversation kept going at this pace, he'd have Jessie's phone number in a matter of minutes. "Maybe I should give her a call, professionally, since I'm almost through with the renovations on my house."

"Not a chance. Aesthetics Ltd. doesn't do domestic interior designs. They work in the corporate sector," he was readily informed.

With a glance at Gary's smirk, Trevor decided to quit while he was ahead. The other man knew exactly what he was doing, and Abby would undoubtedly catch on in a minute. Trevor was satisfied, however, with what he'd managed to find out so far. All he had needed was Jessie's last name, but the name of her business would help if she wasn't listed in the phone book.

"Yoo-hoo, Trevor!"

The sound of Button Mainwairing's shrill voice jerked him to his feet immediately. He would have to worry about his next move with the lovely Jessie later; right now he had to make a hasty escape. He made a quick exit through the Bushes' kitchen door before the female piranha could sink her teeth into him again.

"Okay, I want all the gory details, from the moment he picked you up to the minute he said good-night."

Jessie gave an exasperated sigh as she dropped her purse and portfolio on her glass and chrome desk. She'd expected Gina Caryle to dog her footsteps the moment she entered the office. She also knew Gina wasn't kidding; her friend did want to know *every* detail. It was a miracle that Gina had resisted calling last night. She probably had hoped there was something going on that she might have disturbed.

"He picked me up at seven, and we went to the party," Jessie recited while unbuttoning her cherry-red battle jacket and shrugging out of it. She raised her voice slightly as she crossed the room to where the teapot sat on the black enamel credenza that complemented their ultra-modern office façade. "There were probably forty-five people in various magic-theme costumes, some more interesting than others. We stayed about two and half hours, then he took me home. We said good-night in the car, and I was in bed by eleven."

"Jess-i-ca!" Gina wailed before dropping into the bright yellow acrylic chair by the side of Jessica's desk, crossing her long legs at the knee to show she was settling in for an inquisition that would put Torquemada to shame. "What am I going to do with you? This is the third candidate you've brushed off. How are you ever going to find Mr. Right at this rate?"

Jessie finished pouring her tea and added a packet of sweetener before she bothered to answer. What would Gina's reaction be if she told her about Trevor the rabbit? Studying her friend through half-closed eyes, she shuddered. They'd been friends for too many years, through college and their apprenticeships, for her not to know exactly what the other woman would think—Trevor was wonderful. If Jessie had anything to say about it, Gina would never know about her amorous encounter at the Bushes' party.

"Wait a minute," Jessie answered thoughtfully while walking across the room to take a seat behind her desk. "Aren't you the one who said I was being too cold-blooded about trying to find a husband? I shouldn't make up a list of positive traits and look for a man who fits nine out of ten qualifications?"

"Of course I did. This shopping for a man like an item off the shelf is ridiculous," the brunette acknowledged, flipping her long curly hair over her shoulder and settling her elbows on the desk. Her dark brown eyes never left her partner's face, the direct look almost making Jessie feel guilty about keeping Trevor a secret—almost. "You keep reading all those silly books on how to date, how to meet a man, how to captivate your date, how to be the perfect mate—" Gina broke off, seeming to lose count on her fingers, and threw her hands up in exasperation. "Why not just see if there's an instant-husband-and-father kit on the market? Just add a little water, zap him in the microwave for a minute or so, then presto!"

"Gina, we've been over this already," Jessie said patiently, sipping her tea. "I'm thirty-eight years old, and I want to have a family." Until recently she hadn't even been aware that her biological time clock was ticking, when suddenly it seemed ready to explode. She wanted a baby. "I'm not modern enough to go to a clinic and order an instant father for my child. I want it all. Isn't that modern women's battle cry?"

"At least you haven't totally lost your reason. Artificial insemination is sort of like going to a salad bar to select the father's genes," Gina admitted reluctantly, but she wasn't about to give up her original purpose. "You can't tell me you've come up with any likely candidates with your handy little list either. I didn't meet number three, but one and two both had the personalities of igneous rocks. You're letting your childhood memories skew your judgment."

"That's ridiculous. You and I are simply attracted to different types," Jessie returned hastily. She didn't want to admit that Trevor's easy charm had reminded her of her father's gregarious personality. But a beguiling smile and easy manner just didn't go along with commitment and responsibility. Her child was going to have a quiet, dependable man for a father and a stable home life. "Just because our clients think we look like sisters and we tend to think alike on most matters, it doesn't mean we are going to agree on the right husband. I like your Jeff, but I don't want to marry him."

"You have to admit that Jeff is charming and fun as well as stable and dependable, not to mention supportive," Gina shot back smugly in defense of her husband of four years. She always managed to point out that flaw in Jessie's argument. Jeff Caryle could probably be used as an example of the ideal husband by anyone's measure. He was the exception, not the rule, as far as Jessie was concerned.

"Yes, I do. You found the one-in-a-hundred man who can be frivolous without being a bum," she admitted with a sigh, wishing that the lop-eared image of

Trevor's smiling face hadn't instantly appeared in her mind. Hadn't he haunted her dreams enough?

"So you still haven't told me if candidate number three has any potential," her friend challenged.

Jessie suppressed the urge to ask *"Who?"* Suddenly she couldn't remember anything about the man who had taken her to the Bushes' party, including his name. Although every moment spent with Trevor seemed to be engraved in her memory, she couldn't muster a single image of her date. All she could recall was having a tremendous headache by the end of the evening.

"That bad, was he? Can you even remember his name?" Gina's teasing smile quickly disappeared, making it apparent that Jessie wasn't masking her thoughts. "You can't remember his name, and you thought he was good husband potential. Oh, Jessie, we really need to have a serious talk about this list of yours."

The ringing of the telephone saved Jessie from having to respond immediately. She grabbed the receiver in relief. "Aesthetics, Ltd., Jessica DeLord speaking," she answered over Gina's agonized groan of defeat. "Mr. Planchet has been called out of town? I see. Let me check our schedule for a new date for the presentation." Gina thrust the appointment book into her hand a second later. "How is a week from Monday? Yes, I understand that is a tentative appointment and you'll confirm by the end of the week. Thank you."

"So we don't go up against the big guns for another week. It's almost a relief," Gina murmured as Jessie replaced the receiver. "This way we have more time to practice the presentation."

"It isn't like you to be nervous. You're supposed to be the partner with nerves of steel, remember?" Jessie didn't want to acknowledge the queasy feeling in the pit of her stomach. Another week before facing T. L. Planchet and his board wasn't going to help her sleep.

Sleepless nights tended to make her think of things she'd like to forget, like being kissed by a very sexy rabbit. The rabbit probably wasn't losing any sleep over her.

"It's having to make the presentation to his family as well as the board of directors. The board was in on the initial bid," Gina explained, a frown marking her patrician features, "but the family could have us redesigning the whole scheme for the new office complex. What if the rest of the family is as eccentric as Planchet himself?"

"If we have to redesign, we'll redesign. Mr. Planchet said it was only a formality," Jessie returned in her usual role as placater. T. L. Planchet was renowned for his colorful, larger-than-life personality, though he had seemed to be the personification of a corporate leader during their meetings. "We've already met his son, and he approved of what we've planned."

"I suppose if we can make a stuffed shirt like Sanders Planchet happy, the rest of the family shouldn't be too tough," her partner grudgingly agreed. An evil smile spread across her lips. "Maybe ol' T.L. has another stodgy son who could be a responsible and dependable daddy candidate."

"Cute, Gina, really cute," Jessie murmured, wondering how long it would take for her to forget about Trevor.

_____ TWO _____

"It's now T-minus-five and counting, ladies and gentleman, before the meteoric launch of the fantastic design firm of Aesthetics, Ltd. to stellar heights." Gina's resonant intonation echoed around the rectangular boardroom ten days later. She was occupied with setting up the easel on one side of the room, directly in front of a floor-to-ceiling wall hanging of natural fibers that complemented the tans and browns of the monochromatic decor. The joint owners of Aesthetics, Ltd. had arrived at Planchet Enterprises a good twenty minutes ahead of schedule to prepare for their presentation. "We're bringing you this auspicious meeting from gavel to gavel so you won't miss a single thrill-packed minute of this landmark occasion."

"Will you stop that? You're confusing me as well as your scenarios, and that's the worst Walter Cronkite impression I've ever heard," Jessie chided as she smoothed down the straight skirt of her jade suit, though she appreciated her friend's attempt to distract her from the volcano smoldering in her stomach. Sorting through the drawings, designs, and fabric samples that represented the Planchet project, she acknowledged that this was a landmark day after so many years of dreaming. The Planchet account would be the most prestigious project they had handled thus far.

"Sorry, it was supposed to be Wolf Blitzer," her partner explained without appearing chastened. "Jeff was snuggled up to the TV again this weekend. This is a man who thinks C-SPAN is a mini-series without an ending. His major fault is twenty-four-hour news programs, for you husband hunters. So, add 'no cable news watching' to your list of requirements; it's worse than being a sports widow, at times."

"I'm concentrating on textures and colors for now, thank you very much." That was all Jessie managed before a loud bass voice interrupted them.

"Ladies, darned if you didn't catch me in my shirt sleeves," exclaimed T. L. Planchet, his round face creased by a welcoming smile. He gave his gaudy purple-and-red paisley suspenders a deprecating look that was disarming as he crossed the room with his hand outstretched. Neither of the women had expected him to greet them personally, despite the receptionist's insistence that she announce their arrival.

"Good morning, Mr. Planchet," both Jessie and Gina chorused automatically before shaking hands with their client. Jessie relaxed slightly under the twinkling regard of his brown eyes. The jovial man before them bore little resemblance to the implacable corporate photograph that appeared regularly in *Arkansas Business* and the business section of the *Arkansas Democrat-Gazette*.

"I think our anxiety is showing by arriving ahead of schedule," she found herself admitting. There was something paternal about T. L. Planchet at times, she decided as her partner grimaced over her statement. She simply couldn't be intimidated by a man whose garish suspenders seemed the proper accessory to his charcoal suit pants and blue shirt.

"I admire people who worry about punctuality," he stated heartily. Glancing at his watch, he continued, "I just wish I had taught my own family better. If I had any takers, I'd bet my bottom dollar that two of my children will be late this morning."

"Good morning, Father." Sanders Planchet stepped through the doorway as if on cue. "Ms. DeLord and Ms. Caryle, it is nice to see you again."

"Mr. Planchet," they responded in unison again. Jessie refused to meet Gina's speculative look. Sanders Planchet did look like the epitome of the respectable businessman in his dark blue suit that had clearly been tailored to his stocky figure.

Jessie wasn't, however, going to let her friend's impudent sense of humor relax her guard. Usually she liked a round of nonsensical chatter before a presentation, but today was simply too important. Though she'd dismissed Gina's concern about having to redesign the entire project, she really didn't want to have to rework weeks of preparation.

"Curtiss called a few minutes ago with his excuses, Father." Sanders's grimace and disapproving tone clearly showed his thoughts on the matter. "He claims that he has an emergency to handle at his office. Something about a dog bite."

His father nodded before explaining. "Curtiss, my youngest boy, is a veterinarian, ladies. It must be serious, or he would be here. He and Sanders are the two offspring who can tell time. Now, I think we should get on a first-name basis, so we won't get confused with too many Mr. Planchets. If you don't mind, Jessica and Gina?"

"No, sir," came the dual reply, which had both women smiling self-consciously at continually answering at the same time. Gina nodded her head slightly for Jessie to take the position of spokesperson.

"That would be fine, T.L.," she stated clearly, giving him a polite smile as three members of the board were ushered in by his secretary. Two more arrived a minute later as Jessie and Gina conferred one last time.

"Jessica, we'll go ahead and begin," T.L. prompted a few minutes later from where he stood next to his seat at the center of the table. Though he hadn't bothered to retrieve his suit jacket or roll down his shirt sleeves, he was clearly the man in charge. "As I said earlier, my remaining offspring will undoubtedly be late. Your time is too valuable to waste by waiting on them.

"Ladies and gentleman," he announced to the seven men and four women seated on the far side of the table, "Jessica DeLord and Gina Caryle are here to show us the final plans Aesthetics, Ltd. has made for our new offices. They've discussed the structural plans with Grisham and Collins, and I think y'all will find the results agreeable. Please hold your comments until the presentation is finished. Jessica, let's begin."

Jessie took a deep breath, trying not to think of the twelve people facing her as a hanging jury. Flexing her fingers around her chrome-plated pointer she began describing the decor for the new reception area of the four-story structure. Her level of confidence had surged tenfold by the time she finished describing the area, and Gina smoothly removed the first drawing. This was the day Jessie had been looking forward to during those long nights of waitressing while putting herself through college. At thirty, she'd finally earned her diploma and continued to slave away counting the time until she had the experience and financing to open her own firm. She and Gina had arrived at last.

"Daddy, I'm so sorry we're late. I was on time, but when I picked up Tr—" The dark-haired woman broke off as she caught sight of Jessie to her right and gave her an apologetic smile. "Excuse me for interrupting, I should have known T.L. wouldn't wait for us."

"I should've taken bets, Tory," her father declared as he waved toward a chair on his right. "Now, where's your idiot brother?"

"He's parking the car," she answered quickly, not disputing his description. As she took her seat, she smiled at Jessie once more, regret shining from her brown eyes.

"Not anymore," stated an all-too-familiar voice from the doorway that made Jessie childishly want to hide behind the easel or, better still, disappear into thin air. This couldn't be happening to her; it had to be a bad dream conjured up by Gina's ridiculous comments about T.L.'s sons. Her only rational thought was that now she knew why Tory Planchet looked so familiar; she'd been at the Bushes' party, dressed in a turquoise jumpsuit.

"Please excuse our tardiness, but someone who was the designated driver hadn't bothered to put any gas in her car and expected us to get here on fumes. We wasted precious time changing to my car," Trevor pronounced, sauntering into the room with easy grace. His winsome smile, directed at those seated at the table, seemed to say he knew they would excuse him as a matter of course. Then he turned his attention toward Jessie. "Ms.—Jessie, my Lady of the Legs."

Jessie was sure she could hear the proverbial pin drop as he reached her side in three strides. She was sure her body had turned into one great, big embarrassed stone, if stones could blush, she thought irrelevantly. Trevor dispelled her frozen image by taking her hand and easily raising it to his lips. If she'd had the strength she would have clipped him across the chin. In the back of her mind she could remember her father ruining her eighth birthday party by coming home drunk after being gone for months, smiling ingratiatingly and so earnestly apologetic.

"If I had known you were Daddy's decorator I would have been here an hour early." He simply stood holding her hand, his thumb gently stroking her knuckles, giving no indication of letting her go or moving from her side.

"Trevor, will you try to act like an adult for a change?" his brother snapped, beginning to rise from his chair as if he would physically put the younger man in his place. "You might be at loose ends during the day, but the rest of us have work to get done. Let Ms. DeLord finish her presentation so she doesn't think we're all as mannerless as you and Tory."

Sanders's words acted as an antidote for Jessie's paralysis. She snatched her hand away from Trevor's warm clasp and stepped back. She hoped she appeared to be conferring with Gina about where they had been when interrupted by the late arrivals. No one else heard her partner's bemused whisper, "Who is that masked man?"

"Jessie, if my middle son will cooperate, we'll go ahead with your presentation. Sanders, Trevor, sit." T.L.'s amused gaze belied his terse words, despite the fact Trevor ignored the chair he had indicated. Instead he dropped with a disturbing grace into the chair directly in front of Jessie as his older brother resumed his seat.

Later she was never positive exactly how she managed to say one coherent word, let alone do justice to the proposal for Planchet Enterprises. All she remembered clearly about the next hour were the speculative looks that went from the man in front of her to her rigid figure by the easel. Of those seated at the table, Tory Planchet seemed the most interested. How much did Trevor's sister remember about the Bushes' party?

Ignoring her audience didn't give Jessie any respite. Whenever she glanced in Gina's direction her partner was eyeing the man as if he were her favorite dessert—double dipped in semi-sweet chocolate, rolled in cashews, and topped with whip cream. The only person who seemed unaffected in the aftermath of Trevor's outrageous entrance was Trevor himself.

Like his father, he didn't appear to be bothered by business conventions. He was dressed in slate-blue pleated slacks, the same blue alternating with gray and brown stripes in his shirt. His suspenders, however, were a conservative brown that matched his knit tie. And Jessie had the urge to snap, "Stop that," as he crossed his legs and idly swung his ankle from side to side.

His hooded gaze never strayed to the easel. Instead his attention alternated between her face and her body. For one wild moment, she imagined he was mentally undressing her, then ruthlessly dismissed the thought before she created her own mental image of Trevor dressed only in rabbit ears. Thankfully, Gina uncovered the final drawing, of T.L.'s office, a second later.

When she finished, a polite round of applause from the others was punctuated by shouts of "Bravo" from one of the company. Jessie expelled her breath, relieved she hadn't fainted—yet.

"Jessie, the concept is as delightful as I remember."

T.L. succeeded in drowning out his son with little effort. "Does anyone have any questions or comments?" The question was followed by general murmurings of approval and compliments as the others rose to their feet.

"Are you sure that pink color is going to work in the ladies' restroom off the lobby?"

Jessie kept her smile in place only by biting into the side of her mouth for a moment before she answered. "That pink color is called dusty mauve, Mr. Planchet. It's a very soothing color. I've used it in my own home."

"Really? Where?" Trevor's eyebrows rose in polite inquiry, but his expression told her he was asking ridiculous questions only so she would look at him.

"It's a good choice, Jessie," T.L. said expansively. "You and Gina have excellent color sense. That's one of the reasons I felt Aesthetics, Ltd. was our best choice." He rounded the table, seeming to place himself purposely between Jessie and his son. He couldn't know he saved Jessie from admitting she'd used the disputed color in her bedroom. "Isn't that right, Trev?"

"Yes, sir." Jessie was amazed at his deference to his father, though there had been nothing censuring in his father's tone.

"Good, good, then we're all agreed," the elder Planchet exclaimed, shaking hands with both Jessie and Gina once more as the board members bid them good-bye and left. Minutes later, only the Planchets remained. "If it isn't too much trouble, I would like to keep the drawings for a few days, just to let the staff see what they can look forward to in our new home."

"Certainly, T.L. Keep them as long as necessary," Gina answered when Jessie was suddenly busy rearranging the drawings under discussion and placing them on the long walnut table that bisected the room. "We can't wait to get started on this," she continued as Jessie, overly aware that Trevor was poised for the minute she turned back toward the small group, started to gather up both their purses and the portfolio. "It's going to be such a pleasure working with *all* of you."

Stiffening slightly at her partner's emphasis, Jessie continued to impersonate the anal-retentive decorator until only the coffee cups and waterglasses needed to be cleared away. The rest of her day was going to be a total loss, because she would be fending off Gina's questions.

"Yes, I think this is going to be much more interesting than I anticipated when Daddy asked us to give our seal of approval," Tory Planchet agreed from next to her father. "To think Trevor whined all the way over here. Of course, I had to rouse the beast out of bed, so that might account for it."

"Should I tell Daddy about my little dinner with your Yankee friend while he was away, sister dear?" Trevor asked quietly, but Jessie noticed his sister suddenly seemed to be interested in the pattern of the carpet. Was the Yankee friend the man standing with Trevor by the fig tree that night?

"I think that we're ready to get back to the office, T.L.," Jessie announced brightly, giving Gina "The Look," which had a thousand translations. Today her partner seemed to understand immediately that it meant "Get me out of here now, or I won't be responsible for my actions."

She and Gina murmured a general good-bye. Jessie made sure there was always someone between her and Trevor. She was too drained to deal with whatever nonsense he would begin, undoubtedly some impassioned, but implausible, story about thinking of her for the past week. Men like him were always charming, effusive and full of—

"Trevor, don't take another step. You've done more than enough for one day," she heard Tory say from behind her. Unable to resist, Jessie looked over her shoulder and immediately regretted it. Trevor was staring straight at her, all the former good humor gone from his face. For a fleeting moment her traitorous mind translated the expression as real disappointment. Shaking her head, she turned away to follow Gina to the elevator. Trevor Planchet would hardly be disappointed that she was leaving without speaking to him.

"Trevor Eugene Planchet, you have to be the biggest jerk on the face of the earth," Tory said without moving her lips as she waved to her father before the elevator doors closed.

"Hey, I said I'd let you drive, even if it is my turn to have the T-bird." He wasn't about to admit he knew exactly why his sister was about to read him the riot act. It had nothing to do with their joint ownership of the white 1957 T-bird.

"I should make you walk home. You aren't fit to be out in public with decent people," she continued as if he hadn't said a word. "You've been reading your fan mail again, haven't you? How many times have I told you that you aren't God's gift to women simply because you're on television every day of the week. First it was that poor woman at Abby's party last week, and now this—"

The doors of the elevator opened onto the parking deck and gave him a temporary reprieve as they passed two men getting on. But Trevor knew his sister; she could be as tenacious as a coon dog on the prowl. He held his breath, waiting to see if she would make the connection. He knew she hadn't seen him kiss Jessie that night, but Abby was sure to have filled her in on all the gory details by now.

"How could you embarrass poor Jessica DeLord that way?" Tory renewed her attack as they headed for the car.

"You called her Jessica." He stopped in the middle of the ramp to give her a speculative look. No one had called her Jessica today, had they? She *had* been talking to Abby.

"That's the name on the business card Daddy sent along with his royal summons to this meeting." She shot him a curious look that made him regret his suspicions. "You didn't bother to read the letter, and that's why you were still in bed this morning. Serves you right. So what's the big deal about my knowing her name—"

He knew he was doomed as sudden comprehension crossed his sister's expressive face. Tory hadn't realized earlier that Jessie had been at the Bushes' party, but she knew now.

"Oh, Trev," was all she managed before she doubled over with laughter. As he heard a car approaching from the level above he was tempted not to move his sister out of harm's way. After a moment's hesitation he took her still-convulsed figure by the elbow and steered her out of the path of the oncoming car. Waiting for Tory to become rational again, he glanced idly at the maroon van as it passed.

His heart jumped into his throat as it had in the Planchet Enterprises boardroom an hour earlier. He was looking directly into Jessica DeLord's blue eyes. The woman was beginning to haunt his waking hours as well as his dreams, he decided with a shake of his head. It probably hadn't been her this time, simply his imagination. Without realizing it, he watched the van drive around the curve toward the street level and out of sight.

"Oh, this is incredible."

"Did you say something?" he asked absently. Shoving his hands in his pants pockets, he began walking toward the T-bird parked in its specially reserved place.

"I never thought I'd live to see the day that the mighty Trevor Planchet had fallen, and apparently fallen hard." Tory was laughing again, but this time she had herself under control. She was still giggling as she slipped into the passenger seat.

"What are you nattering about now?" He didn't wait for her answer before starting the car and backing out of the space.

"Jessica DeLord was the woman at the party," Tory stated without hesitation. "Now I understand your performance upstairs. That will teach you not to read one of Daddy's letters. You didn't know she was going to be there until you walked into the room. You've gotten so used to reading from a script that you don't know how to act when faced with the unexpected. I should have recognized your clown mode before this. I must be slipping."

He didn't like the turn in the conversation, or rather, Tory's monologue. If he didn't know why Jessie intrigued him so much, how could he explain it to his sister? This was too much like his conversation with Abby the night of the party. He'd avoided calling Jessie for over a week to see if the fascination with the lady would simply go away. Unfortunately, he'd lain awake every one of those nights wondering how he was going to make up to Jessie for his clumsy behavior. Now he'd made another major faux pas. It was amazing that he could still function with both feet planted firmly in his mouth.

"So, Mr. Stud, how are you going to get yourself out of this one?"

For a minute he didn't realize that Tory had asked the question instead of his subconscious. "Tory, you're creating the most incredible fantasy out of a silly incident. You know the best way to make people forgive your transgressions is to make them laugh. T.L.'s group looked like they'd been taking Sanders-look-alike lessons and needed a good laugh."

"Usually not at someone else's expense, even to get big brother's goat." Tory wasn't laughing any longer, but Trevor could see amusement as well as curiosity lurking in the eyes identical to his own.

"I'll make you a deal. I won't ask you any more embarrassing questions about Logan for a week if you do the same about Jessie," he challenged as he stopped for a red light. The rumble of the idling engine was the only sound in the car for the next few minutes. He knew that Logan Herrington, T.L.'s house guest from Boston, would quickly take Tory's mind off Jessie. Trevor didn't know exactly what had happened between Tory and Logan during the past two weeks, but he had more than a sneaking suspicion she was changing her attitude about Yankees, at least one in particular.

"Dammit, I agree," his sister finally said, grudgingly.

"Spit and rub your heart?"

"Trevor, this is a silk blouse," she complained, wrinkling her nose at his demand for their childhood assurance.

"Wanna talk about you and Logan in a Winnebago on a weekend trip to Oklahoma?" He knew he'd hit pay dirt when Tory's cheeks turned a scarlet hue and she began fidgeting with the armrest. As much as he would like to pursue the topic, he knew it was safer to stop Tory's questions about a certain lady. At least until he had some better answer.

"All right, you pig." She dutifully spit in her hand, more delicately than she had as a child, and rubbed her hand over her heart five times. "It's your turn."

At that moment he would have agreed to jump up and down on one foot whistling "Dixie" with a plastic Hog hat on his head. Now if he could just get Jessie to speak to him in the next week, or ever again.

"Okay, I've kept my word. I haven't mentioned the meeting at Planchet Enterprises all day, or at least you-know-who," Gina declared as she followed Jessie through the front door of her house at six o'clock.

"Relax. Can't you wait until we sit down before you pounce?" Jessie couldn't resist baiting her just a little, since she knew that Gina was going to grill her ruthlessly in a few minutes.

"I'm not sure. After so many hours of self-control I may explode." Gina shrugged out of her coat before dropping limblessly onto the flower-upholstered medallion-backed sofa. "Can I at least say his name now?"

"I said, 'relax,' not 'become comatose.'" Jessie eyed her friend's supine form with a touch of envy. Even after twenty years away from home, she still couldn't abandon herself to complete relaxation. Her mother always taught her that a lady respected her body and didn't act slothful, even if she lived in third-class housing and wore hand-me-down clothes.

"I'm not going to be distracted. I want to know when and how you met Trevor Planchet, one of Little Rock's most eligible bachelors. You can tell me later how you got him wrapped around your little finger when thousands have failed."

"You suddenly know an awful lot about him. Why keep it a secret until now?"

"Secret? You're accusing me of secrets? I figured you knew." Her look of astonishment only added to Jessie's confusion. Before she could ask what she was supposed to know, Gina groaned in frustration and jumped to her feet. When she walked to the ornate armoire at the end of the room, opened the doors, and turned on the television, Jessie was thoroughly bewildered.

"I thought Jeff was the news junky."

"He is, but I'm a sports groupie along with thousands of other women across the state," Gina said in exasperation. "I guess I should be glad your television works, since you rarely watch it."

"Gina, what *are* you doing?"

"Shush."

"Now let's find out what the Hawg forecast is going to be, folks," proclaimed the perfectly coiffed newsman. "What are our chances in the play-offs, Trev?"

"Well, Ted, it's going to be another cliffhanger this year for the Hawg fans," Trevor Planchet proclaimed, his lazy smile filling the television screen, "but the Arkansas State alums have some cheering to do."

"Criminy, he's on the news? That's why he was asleep at nine o'clock in the morning." Jessie couldn't believe what she was seeing. Trevor was in a suit jacket and tie, smoothly reporting the latest developments in the sports world. For a moment, she wondered if he had a double that could look like a respectable human being.

"I call it the Four-T Report—Ted, Tina, Trixie, and Trevor," Gina informed her, lowering the volume but not bothering to turn off the set. She had a smug smile on her face as she returned to the couch. "And, yes,

Trixie reports the weather, but I don't think that's why your mouth is hanging open.''

"It must have been the rabbit ears," she murmured without realizing it. As Gina said, Jessie rarely watched television except for vintage movies and AETN, the state's PBS network, but she must have seen Trevor sometime before last week. She wasn't that closed off from the outside world. Or was she?

"Rabbit ears? Is this going to be kinky?" The avid look on Gina's face made Jessie bury her face in her hands, groaning and considering the fetal position for the rest of the evening. "You promised me the whole story if I wouldn't mention this morning's performance until after we left work. I'm abandoning my husband to a solitary night, the poor baby, just so I can find out what in the Sam Hill is going on."

"The poor baby plays poker every Monday night." Jessie reluctantly raised her head, knowing she couldn't procrastinate any longer. "Remember the Bushes' party?"

"He couldn't have been candidate number three. You would have remembered *his* name without any trouble."

"Of course he wasn't. He wouldn't even qualify for a single category on my list." Jessie gave a snort of derision, though she had anticipated Gina's reaction accurately.

"Yes, he would. His salary and family background would make him a shoe-in on the financial question."

Jessie told Gina as quickly and as succinctly as possible everything that had taken place—well, almost everything. She couldn't quite bring herself to talk about the farewell kiss. That incident was still haunting her dreams.

"You mean you tossed aside a piece of prime beefcake like Trevor Planchet for this reject lawyer?"

"How did you ever marry someone as nice as Jeff? By rights you deserve some airhead who postures in front of a mirror twenty-four hours a day," Jessie exclaimed, wondering if she was ever going to convince Gina that she was right about her ideal husband. "Appearances aren't everything."

"And every handsome man with a charming smile isn't a reprobate. We both agree your father was a suave good-for-nothing that left your mama and his family to shift for themselves," Gina stated without rancor as a long-time friend. "Do you think you'll be able to trust any of your candidates enough to marry one of them? There's no guarantee when it comes to relationships."

"I won't know until I find the right candidate, but I'm making sure the odds are much better by looking for a man who understands responsibility." She glanced at the television screen again just as the camera pulled back to show the entire news team as the credits rolled. The Four-Ts, as Gina had dubbed them, were doing happy talk as the theme music swelled. "I don't think Trevor Planchet has a responsible bone in his body. Not the man who disrupted our meeting this morning as a ploy to dismiss his tardiness, or the man who kissed—"

"He kissed you? Sometimes I have the juvenile urge to give you a good swift kick in the tush." She swung her feet to the floor, sitting up almost as primly as Jessie. "Is there any more that you've been too scared to tell me about Trevor Planchet?"

"Scared? You do have a vivid imagination at times." Jessie tried to ignore the shiver that skated down her spine. Was she afraid to talk about Trevor? Certainly not. She didn't mention him before today because she knew that Gina would exaggerate everything totally out of proportion. Hadn't Gina dressed her up in that outlandish outfit because of some wild romantic thought that Jessie might find, what was it Gina had said earlier, a piece of prime beefcake to sweep her off her feet?

Jessie knew better. That only happened in books and the movies. In real life, you had to worry about getting food on the table, mortgage payments, and new pairs of shoes for the kids. Those things weren't paid for by a man who dressed up in rabbit ears, even if he did call her his Lady of the Legs, she decided, unconsciously studying her ankle as she moved her foot back and forth.

THREE

"Can I interest you in watching me eat some humble pie?"

Jessie swayed for a moment near the top of the stepladder at the sound of Trevor's voice from close to her feet. She juggled the cumbersome book of wallpaper samples in her hands for a moment before shoving it back on the shelf. Maybe this was another of her recurring nightmares from the past two days. Or maybe not, she admitted reluctantly and looked down.

He was leaning against the metal shelving lining the other side of the storage area. For a minute she wondered if the somber man regarding her was the same Trevor Planchet who'd been disturbing her peace of mind for almost two weeks. He seemed to have changed personalities with his solemn older brother, even dressing more conservatively in a tattersall plaid shirt and gray slacks. This certainly wasn't the grinning satyr that had been disturbing her dreams.

"How did you get back here?" Her tone was sufficiently neutral, she decided, since his dour expression made her uneasy. Keeping a wary eye on him she stepped carefully down the three steps to the carpeted floor. A ladder was hard enough to maneuver in her teal jersey sheath without Trevor watching her descent. This wasn't the time to do something absurd, like fall at his feet.

"Your partner said you were back here working on the inventory." He didn't move from his negligent position, almost as if he was reluctant to startle her with any sudden movement. "I brought back your drawings and samples from Daddy's office."

"I see." Of course, Gina had told him exactly where she was. Her romance-minded partner probably thought they would enact some scene out of a Doris Day movie. Jessie would lose her balance at Trevor's first words, then he would catch her and hold her to his manly chest. Unfortunately, the silly idea brought to mind an accurate image of Trevor's naked chest. She could feel a tingling sensation all the way down to her stockinged feet, making her wonder suddenly what the devil she'd done with her shoes.

"Look—"

"I have—"

Both of them broke off together, then waited. Neither seemed to know where to begin again. Trevor nodded his head in deference to her.

"Thank you for bringing back our materials. We're getting ready for the spring samples to arrive, and I'm right in the middle of this inventory. . . ." She let the words drift away for lack of anything else that wouldn't sound impolite. By tactfully choosing her words she hoped to avoid any more of his histrionics.

"Would you have lunch with me? That's really why I volunteered for messenger duty," he explained, no trace of emotion in his tone or his expression. When Jessie started to form another excuse, he held up his hand. "I really would like to apologize for what happened at the meeting as well as at the Bushes' party.

Sometimes the Planchets get a little overdramatic without thinking about the consequences. I don't seem to be able to carry it off with the same savoir faire as T.L. He's called eccentric, and I'm labeled obnoxious.''

''An apology really isn't necessary.'' The last thing she wanted to do was spend time alone with Trevor. It would be total insanity. ''These things happen and life goes on.''

''You probably think having lunch would be dangerous,'' he continued, shifting his feet restlessly from side to side, unaware that he was mirroring her thoughts. ''But I promise that I won't do anything crazy, like burst into song or make rude noises.''

''Really, Trevor—''

''She'd love to go to lunch after being cooped up back in this dusty old storage room for hours,'' Gina broke in, startling the two. She ignored Jessie's fulminating glare and handed her her shoes before she continued. ''A nice lunch would be perfect way to let Trevor apologize, wouldn't it, Jessie? Didn't I just say the other day that you don't get out enough? The business is taking up too much of your free time.''

Jessie wanted to tell her partner exactly what she thought would be perfect while trying to maintain her dignity as she slipped into her cream-and-teal spectators. Then, as she straightened and noticed Trevor's interested expression, decided against saying what was on her mind. She was at a loss as to how to avoid going to lunch with the man. Gina's chatter made it clear that Trevor's behavior on both occasions was general knowledge, so Jessie couldn't act as if the incidents had been trivial.

''All right, lunch it is.'' Her softly spoken words caught the others unaware, which gave Jessie a small sense of satisfaction. She would devise a suitable revenge for her manipulative friend later, when she had time to create something truly diabolical. ''I'll just get my purse and jacket. Where would you like to go, Trevor?''

"How about that little café down near the Old State House?" he asked as he followed her out of the storage room.

Jessie knew she was going to regret this, even without seeing the pleased smiles on Trevor's and Gina's faces as they hovered by her desk.

"Now, see, that wasn't so bad." Trevor leaned back in his chair as the waiter cleared away their dishes. Lunch had gone fairly well, even if he did think so himself. Over spinach salads and shrimp bisque soup, they'd talked amicably about the upcoming election as well as other current events. "You didn't have to be afraid of coming out with me."

He knew he'd said the wrong thing before the words were even out of his mouth. Helplessly he watched Jessie's eyes flash blue fire in irritation, though she continued to sip her iced tea. His entire body tensed as she very carefully placed the glass back on the salmon-colored linen tablecloth. Damn, she was stunning when she was angry, her eyes sparkling and a flush coloring her porcelain skin.

"Look, that's not what—"

"Trevor, I wasn't afraid to come to lunch with you." Her words were softly spoken and apparently selected with great care. He watched in fascination as she wet her lips before continuing. "I don't think we have very much in common. Your personality doesn't mesh well with mine. We're as different as night and day. That's all."

That wasn't all, or she wouldn't be trying to control her temper. Her willowy body was perfectly stiff, posture perfect. She couldn't keep her fingers from straightening the silverware or from making sure an errant strand of raven hair hadn't escaped her French plait, just as she had done when they first sat down. This cool and competent lady wasn't ruffled when he'd disrupted her business meeting or when faced with her lunkhead date's officious manner. Yet with him she was always on guard, as if keeping a more passionate side of her nature under control. Was that what continued to captivate him?

Damned if he wasn't going to find out, no matter what the consequences. He'd been playing tame eunuch for two hours for nothing. Getting Jessie riled and off balance was the key.

"So I take it your deadwood escort at the Bushes' party *is* your type," he blurted out, sitting forward to lean his forearms on the table. "I would think a stunning woman like you could do much better. What was his name? Kirby, Conrad?"

"Tr—Trevor, who I date really isn't important." Her cheeks were turning a deeper shape of pink, and she wouldn't meet his eyes. "It's all really a matter of personal taste. I wouldn't think of questioning you about your private life."

"But I find this interesting," he said, *especially that you can't remember his name, either,* he finished silently, fighting a smug smile. Apparently something, or someone, had erased the jerk from her memory. He also noted with satisfaction that she hadn't corrected his description of the man.

"He—he was simply a convenient escort for the occasion," she finally managed, her agitation over the matter out of proportion. She was as much aware of it as he was. "Does that satisfy your curiosity?"

"Yes, ma'am," he said simply as the waiter handed him his credit card and receipt.

"Thank you for lunch, Trevor. I think this has been a suitable apology for our earlier mishaps. Now I must return to the office." Jessie had her hands primly folded over her discarded napkin, which she had neatly creased back into its original shape.

He wondered if she knew she started talking like Queen

Victoria when she was upset. Did she stay that prim and proper when she was making love? A truly interesting concept, he decided, rising to his feet to follow her out of the restaurant and out onto the sidewalk.

"You don't have to walk me back to the office. It's only a few blocks from here." Jessie looked as if she was prepared to run the entire way if necessary.

"Nonsense, Jessie." He cupped her elbow with the proper degree of pressure, not too impersonal but enough to keep her at his side as he guided her down the busy thoroughfare. "I would be drummed out of the Southern gentlemen's club if I didn't escort a lady to her door. This may be the age of the independent woman, but that doesn't mean courtesy has to be thrown out the window. Don't you agree?"

He couldn't clearly interpret the message from her grinding teeth, but he was sure if she managed a verbal answer it would be negative. Unfortunately, for her, the same good manners he used in his defense were working against her. She had to let him walk her back to her office, but apparently she didn't have to talk to him. That didn't bother Trevor. He kept up a steady commentary about the current weather, forecasting the next rainfall.

"Thank you again, Trevor." She ground out the words from behind a plastic smile, her right foot poised on the first step into the building.

Trevor slid his hand down from her elbow to capture her hand. She was caught, unless she wanted to play an undignified tug-of-war in front of the other pedestrians returning from lunch. He placed his index finger against her lips before she had a chance to speak.

"I think it's only fair to tell you that I usually get what I want, Jessie. I also love a challenge." He accentuated his meaning by gently tugging on her hand. That was all it took to tumble her into his arms.

Her lips tasted sweeter than he remembered, but he

didn't allow himself to linger. If he did, he'd have her down on the pavement in a matter of minutes. He wanted to entice Jessie, not get her arrested for indecent exposure.

Placing his hands on her shoulders, he turned her around and gave her a mild nudge up the steps toward the door of the building. He knew he had to make a clean getaway before his delightful Jessie could retaliate. He'd started the day planning to apologize for one kiss, now he had stolen his second. But this time he wasn't a damn bit sorry. Not after he'd seen the slumberous look in Jessie's beautiful eyes before he'd turned away.

All he had to do now was figure out his next step.

Jessie stared moodily at the silk-screened print of San Francisco row houses behind her desk. Usually, dreaming about owning and decorating her own Victorian house soothed her, but not today. The image of Trevor's smiling face just before he left her an hour ago kept superimposing itself over the buildings.

Life just wasn't fair, she decided. Why did all the good-looking rogues have to be irresponsible and capricious? Was it genetic?

Muted chimes announced that someone had walked through the front door, and she swung her chair around to face her desk.

"Mmm, it doesn't look like lunch went very well."

Jessie returned her partner's frown with one of her own. "It depends on your point of view."

"Ohh, judging from your scowl, Trevor must have had a fantastic time," Gina exclaimed, breaking into a smile. Then she seemed to remember that she was supposed to be sympathetic to her friend's plight. "Want to tell me all about it? Cry on Gina's shoulder?"

"I liked your natural reaction better. You need to work on the compassionate care-giver persona for another year or so to be convincing." She propped her chin in her hand to prepare for the barrage of questions that were sure to come.

"I have a very empathetic nature," Gina assured her, trying to maintain her solemn demeanor and failing miserably. The laughter trembling on her lips burst forth. "Just don't tell anyone because it's buried way deep inside. You really can't expect me to be a hypocrite about Trevor. You know exactly what I think on the matter."

"Yes, I know." She liked her friend just the way she was, except when her romantic inclinations overcame her usual pragmatic, straight-to-the-point nature. "I guess you're going to want a play-by-play before I'll be able to get any work done on the estimate for Garrison's tax office."

Gina suddenly found her fingernails fascinating. She seemed preoccupied with checking her cuticles, and it sent a chill of apprehension down Jessie's spine. Biting her lip, she waited for what her partner was going to say.

"Not if it's any more interesting than a certain tender farewell, right in front of God and everybody." She continued to hold out her hand, but Jessie could see her looking surreptitiously through her eyelashes.

"Harvey in the print shop on the first floor." In her mind's eye, Jessie could picture the biggest gossip on the block watching the whole episode. The entire south corner of the building was plate glass, which gave Harvey Milsap a perfect view of everything that happened on two sides of the office building. He was more reliable than reading the news, since he even reported what wasn't fit to print.

"Harvey said it was simply stunning, like a Joan Crawford or Bette Davis melodrama. It sent chills down his spine. Of course, Harvey just loves a forceful man." Gina looked thoughtful for a moment as she eyed Jessie's teal-and-cream herringbone jacket. "Maybe you should get rid of those shoulder pads."

"That's all you have to say?" Jessie knew better, but thought she would ask anyway.

"When are you going to have a real date with Trevor?"

"He didn't ask me out." Jessie had the satisfaction of saying it, only she wasn't happy about the feeling of chagrin that returned as she admitted it. It was stupid, but she'd felt disappointed that he hadn't asked for a date after that kiss.

Telling herself that she was disappointed simply because she hadn't had the pleasure of turning him down didn't work. That kiss had been more than a simple good-bye. Her legs had barely carried her up the three steps to the entrance and through the door. Thankfully he hadn't seen her slump against the wall to regain her composure just after she'd entered the building.

"How odd," Gina murmured absently, undoubtedly trying to figure out an answer to the puzzle. She couldn't possibly be reading Jessie's mind.

"I keep telling you that rogues like Trevor defy logic, or at least they think they do." Jessie leaned back in her chair, feeling secure in her knowledge of this particular subject.

"But you understand them?" The other woman looked skeptical but anxious to hear what she had to say.

"Just a little. They live by their own rules. Rule number one is their own pleasure. That's the prime directive and takes precedence over everything else."

"Wouldn't a date be pleasurable?"

"Not if he could derive more pleasure by making the lady overly anxious for his company. It's kind of a Big-Man-on-Campus philosophy," she explained, warming to her subject. "He knows he's charming and in demand, so he lets the victim feel privileged to be in his company. To increase the victim's feeling of importance, he plays hard to get. Ergo, he attains more pleasure by feeling twice as worshiped.''

''I don't believe this.'' Gina planted her hands on her hips and began tapping her foot. ''I'm actually listening to some of that pop-psychology you've been inhaling to create Robo-husband, aren't I?''

''It makes perfect sense if you keep an open mind,'' Jessie called after her as Gina stomped away toward her drawing board.

''Yes, one of us should keep an open mind. It could be that the man is going out of town to cover the basketball play-offs this weekend.'' She turned around with a triumphant smile at her sudden inspiration. ''I remember the Four-T's discussing it last night. He isn't going to be in town, so naturally he couldn't ask you out.''

Suddenly Jessie felt a surge of hyperactivity. It had nothing to do with the curl of pleasure in her abdomen at the mention of Trevor's busy schedule, she told herself fiercely and got up to finish the inventory. She had to keep busy this afternoon. The Garrison estimate could be done at home, since she didn't have any other plans. Tossing old pattern books and carpet samples around was just what she needed to relieve her frustrations and keep her mind on her work.

''Tory, I need your help.'' Trevor didn't bother to wait for his sister's greeting after she picked up the phone.

''Why?'' she asked in a groggy voice.

''Don't worry, it isn't illegal or immoral,'' he assured her with a chuckle. Of course, if she even guessed his purpose, she would refuse. But then she didn't know that Jessie DeLord had a penchant for Victorian decor. He'd only learned it this afternoon when he visited her office and saw the pictures and bric-a-brac among the potted plants and the ultra-modern decor.

"Okay, what is it?" she demanded with a sister's impatience.

"Who do I contact about the Quapaw Quarters Tours?"

"What?"

He held the phone away from his ear at her shriek of surprise. House tours in Little Rock's historic area apparently were not what Tory expected. "You remember the annual spring tours of the Quapaw Quarter?" he asked. "You did some catering for them last year, didn't you?"

"Yes, but why do you want to know, and at eleven-thirty at night?"

"Since I'm finally almost finished with the renovations, I thought I might offer my house for the Candlelight Tour. They did a piece on one of the old homes tonight on the news."

"Call the Villa Marre, dumbie. You know the house they film on "Designing Women" for Julia Sugarbaker's home and design firm? It's only a few blocks from where you live." He held his breath in case Tory made the design connection, but he relaxed again when she continued speaking. "The Quapaw Quarter Association headquarters is there. Somebody there can tell you who is chairing the tours this year."

"Great." He wrote down the information, smiling foolishly in anticipation.

"Is that all you wanted?" she asked abruptly.

"Yeah, that's it. I'm taking off tomorrow for the play-off games in Washington, D.C., and wanted to get this done before I left," he assured her, wondering if he could just hang up before he blurted out his brilliant plan.

"Can I go now, Trev?" She was past losing patience with him.

"Say good-night to Logan for me, will ya, Tor?" He had no idea if he was making a wild guess or not, but it would make his sister mad enough not to think about this phone call later. Her only answer was the crack of her receiver being slammed into place.

Maybe he had made a lucky guess, he thought with a shrug as he hung up more gently. He'd worry about Tory and her Yankee later; right now he had more important matters to consider.

He'd ridden a euphoric high for hours after leaving Jessie, only to lose his edge the second he got to work and remembered his trip out of town. Basketball was the last thing he wanted to think about. How was he going to keep her thinking about him if he was over a thousand miles away? He was still worrying over the situation when Tina did a piece on one of the old houses that had been part of a legal battle recently, and suddenly he thought of his solution.

While he'd been waiting in Jessie's office he had idly noticed a number of Richard DeSpain's pen-and-ink drawings of the older homes in Little Rock as well as pictures displaying Victorian architecture in other cities. His Jessie was a decorator, so wouldn't she be willing to decorate a newly renovated home in the Quarter? His intuition told him he was on the right track, especially if the house was going to be part of the annual tours. A decorator wouldn't be able to resist the lure of showing off her work, would she?

Hopefully not Jessica DeLord, he determined, looking around at his bedroom's Spartan furnishings. When he'd inherited the house from his great-aunt, he'd put the furniture worth saving in storage. All he had now was a bed, dresser, a nightstand, and a trunk with a television set on it. Jessie would be able to furnish the entire place. A decorator's dream, he was sure. If that didn't work, he would have to devise another plan when he got back from Washington.

"Did I just hear you accept a date?" Gina asked with suspicion as she walked out of the storeroom after lunch. "Trevor only left town three days ago."

"And?" Jessie couldn't wait to hear this rationale.

"You should be ashamed of yourself."

"For what? Trevor Planchet is simply a man I've seen three times," she returned, wondering what interesting plans her friend had been dreaming up. "You aren't seriously suggesting that I'm betraying him."

"Well, no," Gina had the grace to admit, "but I would think candidate number four will be awfully dull after Trevor. Is this one another lawyer?"

"No, I don't want to take another chance on the legal profession right now. Wes is an accountant—" Jessie didn't get a chance to say any more because Gina's laughter drowned her out.

"Poor number four doesn't stand a chance," she sputtered, then started to laugh once more. When she could speak again, she barely managed, "An accountant? Does he wear a bow tie and a nerd pack?"

"He's six-foot-two, weighs one hundred and ninety pounds, and works out four times a week," Jessie informed her, not able to suppress her smirk. "Remember, if stereotypes were factual, we'd be two gay men."

"Okay, that was nasty. Where did you pick up this one?" Her tone implied that Jessie had been trolling the gutters.

"I met him at the health club, that's why I know how much he weighs." She was saved from hearing Gina's retort by the sound of the door chimes. They both turned to see a slim, older woman entering the office. Automatically Jessie and Gina moved toward the sitting room area at the front of the office. Their visitor was glancing around with a curious look on her face.

"Hello, I'm Jessie DeLord and this is Gina Caryle, partners at Aesthetics, Ltd. How can we help you?" Jessie thought the woman looked familiar but couldn't quite place her.

"Oh, I am in the right place, then. I'm Marquerite Langford-Hughes," she explained, offering a slender, perfectly manicured hand. Her slender face was still marred by a look of consternation.

Returning Mrs. Langford-Hughes's handshake, Jessie exchanged "The Look" with Gina. They were in the presence of one of Little Rock's social elite. The lady was involved in every important charity function in the city, a perennial personality on the society pages of the newspaper. If the Langford-Hugheses weren't at a function, then it wasn't important. Old money was on both sides of the family for generations. What had Aesthetics, Ltd. done to deserve this?

"I'm sorry for just barging in like this, but time is so short," the lady announced, her smile genuine. "I've so much to do in the next few weeks, and now this has come up."

"Won't you sit down, Mrs. Langford-Hughes, and we can discuss this over a cup of tea?" Jessie indicated the royal-blue leather couch as Gina scurried to the credenza.

"Thank you, my dear, that's just what I need. I've been running around all morning." She stepped gingerly over to the couch and sat down, looking almost surprised at the comfort of the couch. "But I'm such a scatterbrain. You have no idea why I'm here, do you?"

"No, ma'am." Jessie sat in the chair next to her just as Gina returned with the tea tray. Jessie was finding the suspense building about this mysterious visit as she helped her partner serve tea.

"What a lovely tea service. Is it a family piece?" Mrs. Langford-Hughes inquired as Gina placed the teapot back on the tray.

"Yes, it's been in my husband's family for years. It was a wedding present from his grandmother," Gina responded with pride. "I believe it's a Tiffany design from the 1870s."

"I think I'm beginning to understand now. The modern office furnishings threw me for a moment," their visitor declared, her glance taking in the various pictures on the wall. Then she burrowed in her oversized purse for a packet of papers that was sandwiched between two pieces of cardboard. "You don't just do contemporary decor."

"Most of our corporate clients prefer it," Gina responded, sounding as if they worked with every major corporation in central Arkansas. "We do like to work with any client's preference, however."

Jessie shrugged as Gina gave her a questioning look. She didn't have the foggiest idea where this interview was heading. At least it seemed to be an interview for a commission.

"I should get to the point and not keep you young ladies from your other business." She drew the rubber band off the packet in her hand as she spoke. "I'm chairing the Quapaw Quarter Tours this spring, which I'm sure you're familiar with. We've been handed such a plum for the Candlelight Tour this year, even if it was at the last minute. The Dalrymple house is in the process of being completely renovated, and your firm was suggested as the decorator."

"We were?" Jessie and Gina chorused, amazed at what had been said.

"Yes, the only catch is the house needs to be com-

pletely done, as you can see from these photographs,''
she explained and handed them pictures that depicted
exterior shots and each of the house's eleven rooms.
"I understand there are a few family pieces in storage,
but most of the furniture will have to be ordered. The
only thing that has been done so far are the hardwood
floors. The place needs drapes, wallpaper, paint, who
knows what else.''

"Oh, Jess, it has a gazebo." Gina handed her the
picture and eagerly took another from Mrs. Langford-
Hughes. "This place is incredible.''

"I know, but can we do it?" Jessie could just picture
what she would do with the dining room. The house
was an early Queen Anne embellished by shingle work
and more ornate Eastlake cutwork on the cantilevered
tower and the trim across the front of the house and
central gable. The porch that ran across the front of the
house and down one side possessed turned posts and
balusters as well as a turret roof in one corner. Work
had already begun on scraping away old paint to give
the exterior a much-needed face-lift.

"Not 'we,' you,'' her partner replied. "Except for
my family heirlooms, I don't know half of what you
do about Victorian interiors. This would be great practice for your dream house. You've always said you
wanted to get involved with the tours anyway.''

"Lovely. Then, it's settled,'' Mrs. Langford-Hughes
declared before delving into her purse to pull out a
legal-sized envelope. "Here are the keys. The owner
is out of town but did say that you should go ahead
with measurements and whatnot and have the contract
ready next week. The house will have to be ready by
the first weekend in May, so time is of the essence.''

"But, Mrs. Langford-Hughes—''

"Don't worry, my dear, you'll do just fine. You
came with a high recommendation from the owner.''

The lady rose majestically to her feet with the pronouncement and headed for the door. "I really must dash now. I have a meeting at Children's Hospital in ten minutes. So nice to meet you; I'll be in touch."

"But, Mrs. Langford—" But the woman was out the door, oblivious to Jessie's voice. "This is strange. I thought she might be here about Symphony House, but it's the wrong time of year," she murmured, dropping back into her chair. The fund raiser sponsored by the Symphony had a different design firm do each room of the house, but that was in the fall of each year.

She never expected to hear about the Quapaw Tours. The residential area immediately east and south of downtown Little Rock represented most of the architectural styles from the early 1800s to post World War II, including the Governor's Mansion. During the last thirty years, local residents had been slowly reclaiming the area that took its name from the Quapaw Line, a geographic division to separate the settlers from the native Quapaw Indians' lands. The Quapaw Quarter tours had become an Event, especially the gala Candlelight Tour.

"Don't look a gift horse in the mouth."

"Gift horse? Did you hear what she said? I have less than six weeks to do an entire house," Jessie said in wonder, trying not to look at the photographs, "if I take the job."

"You're a fool not to do it. We don't start the physical work on Planchet Enterprises until mid-June." Gina began tallying their clients on her fingers. "Garrison's is only at the estimate stage along with Devon's Jewels. We're just finishing up the other three jobs. Can you really resist this tower, plus a turret in the back, and all that beautiful woodwork?"

"No, I can't," she admitted in defeat. This was going to be a lot of extra work, but she would love every minute of it. By keeping her schedule busy she also wouldn't have time to think about Trevor Planchet. He would be out of sight and out of mind for good. She would have a lovely house to decorate and would be able to get on with the business of finding a father for her future child.

FOUR

"This place is absolutely wonderful!" Gina exclaimed while turning in a complete circle to inspect the entry hall of the Dalrymple house. They had not been able to visit the house for two days after Mrs. Langford-Hughes's visit but had finally cleared their schedules for this afternoon.

"You've only seen two rooms and the front porch." Jessie couldn't contain her amusement, acknowledging for perhaps the hundredth time that her friend's impetuous nature helped their partnership work as well as their friendship. She tempered Jessie's more cautious mind. Gina, however, wasn't exaggerating this time, she decided, walking through the walnut-trimmed archway into the large living room area. The owner had worked very carefully to preserve the original woodwork and decorative features in the house.

"Come on out here." Gina's excitement seemed to have increased tenfold. "You aren't going to believe this."

Jessie followed the sound of her voice through the dining room, pausing to admire the newly polished brass chandelier before stepping through the wide doorway that led to the back of the house. What had once been a parlor in the back turret had been converted into a den across from an informal dining area and the modernized kitchen. "What has captured your fancy now? It took me ten minutes to get you off the glider on the front porch to come inside."

Gina was standing one level below her near the sliding glass door that overlooked the backyard. As she went down the four steps to the next level, Jessie could tell from the new flooring and absence of ornate woodwork at the windows and baseboards that the two rooms at the back had been added.

"Get a load of this," Gina said. "I don't think any Victorian had this in mind."

Her partner's lips were twitching as she gestured to an area at the left. At a single glance, Jessie knew why. Victorian morals certainly would not have approved of the sauna that was nestled in the small room that opened onto the back deck. She was pleased with the owner's sense of style in combining the old and new without compromising the integrity of the house.

"That wasn't in any of the pictures," Jessie commented dryly, already selecting decorative plants and considering a stained-glass skylight in the ceiling. Then she opened the sliding glass door that led out onto the wooden deck and stepped outside.

From the front of the house there had been no sign of recent construction. The owner had complemented the earlier period here as well. A planked deck ran along the back of the house from the end of the original porch, then jutted out to the left, leaving two thirds of the rectangular yard to frame the gingerbread carvings of the gazebo in the back. Only a two-story garage remained. At one time there had undoubtedly been other outbuildings. From the smell of new wood, the deck and fence that encircled the yard for privacy had been the most recent additions.

"I think I'm in love." Jessie let out an ecstatic sigh, sinking down onto the top step that led down from the deck to the yard, which was in the process of being landscaped. "This is going to be a fantastic job. Can I stop doing everything else and just move in here for the duration?"

"Fat chance."

"Somehow I knew you'd say that," Jessie returned good-naturedly. They had taken on two more clients in the past few days, one who had been recommended by a member of Planchet Enterprises' board. With the recent upsurge in business, they finally were planning to hire a part-time employee to handle their mounting paperwork.

"I might be open to a bribe, however." Her partner sounded just a little too eager to have her palm crossed with silver. Jessie didn't trust her one bit.

"So what is your price, my avaristic friend?"

"Ah, you can afford me. All you have to do is talk to Trevor the next time he calls," Gina stated, giving her friend a stern look. "He's been chalking up a lot of long-distance charges by calling you in the middle of the day from Washington, and with no result. Why not cut him some slack?"

"Why?" Jessie didn't think she needed any further defense of her actions. Trevor had called twice. Both times she had refused point blank to take the calls, though Gina had been very chatty. There wasn't any point for Jessie to encourage him. He did not fit into her plans. Her dinner two nights ago with Wes Lendall had been very pleasant, proving to her, if not Gina, that her plan of finding a husband had potential.

"Well, your thirty-ninth birthday isn't that far away, ya know," Gina commented, as if she had telepathy.

"So you really shouldn't eliminate too many candidates. That little clock is steadily going *tick-tock, tick-tock.*" Her sound effect was closer to a time bomb than a clock, to Jessie's ears. "This Wes person may seem nice now, but maybe he's a latent ax murderer."

"You have a very strange mind. I think your Trevor would be a better possibility for that job." *Of course, he does kiss better than Wes,* a wicked voice from her subconscious taunted. Jessie shook her head to dispel the idea. Wes had been a perfect gentleman, giving her a mild, proper good-night kiss—highly appropriate for a first date. She really had no right to make a comparison.

"I think you need to exorcise your ghosts before you commit yourself to a serious relationship." The solemn tone of Gina's words took Jessie by surprise. "You're punishing Trevor for something that he hasn't done. He isn't the scoundrel that hurt you and your family, Jessie. And you're not your mother, either."

"Pardon?" She was stunned by the turn in the conversation.

"Just something I picked up from one of your dreadful how-to books the other day while you were at lunch. You've been concentrating on the qualities of your future husband but ignoring a few chapters that dealt with childhood experiences that can color your—what was it?—oh, color your adult interpersonal experiences."

"Are you saying that, due to my parents' relationship, I'll be a lousy wife and mother?"

"Not at all. If that were true, I wouldn't have ever gotten married, what with both my parents each being divorced twice." Gina placed a comforting hand on her partner's knee. "I think you'll be terrific at anything you want to do. You are much stronger than your mother. Remember, she let your father come back time and time again. She forgave him over and over because she loved him and didn't know what else to do. Maybe if she'd given him a good swift kick now and then things might not have been so tragic later. Or maybe not. But I don't think you would continue in a relationship with a man who showed up only every three or four months just to take all your money and disappear again."

"This lecture is so I'll talk to Trevor the next time he calls?" Jessie gave her friend a searching look. They had little time for heart-to-heart talks anymore. When they had been in college together, they had spent many a long night solving the problems of the world as well as their personal problems while dreaming about forming their partnership. Older than most of the students, they had depended on each other.

"Not really. I think this applies to all the daddy candidates," Gina answered decisively. "I was wary of Jeff when we first met, and I wasted two-and-a-half years before he convinced me to marry him, remember? Now, enough of this gloom-and-doom stuff. It might be all academic about Trevor. He might not bother to call again, and we have measurements to take before we leave."

Jessie didn't answer as she rose to her feet. Why should the thought of Trevor giving up depress her? She was well rid of him. It made about as much sense as turning on the pre-game show to the basketball play-off last night. Wouldn't Gina have a field day with that piece of news? she wondered morosely, following her into the house. Gina knew that Jessie loathed basketball.

Jessie was humming along with an old Chicago song as she pulled her car into the Dalrymple house's driveway a week later. Though she'd had a long day, she wanted to see if the green floral fabric she'd found this afternoon for the back turret bedroom would be too dark in artificial light. Once that was done, she could head home to take a soothing bath and slip into her sweats.

With a frustrated sigh, she wished that the owners would come home soon. Picking out two or three fabric alternatives for each room was double the work. Did they want contemporary, true Victorian, or a mixture of both? However, she had to admit that delving into the various patterns and styles kept her mind from wandering down dangerous paths.

Still humming, she slung her tote bag over her shoulder and headed for the front steps. She didn't notice the dim light from inside the house until she reached the porch. Maybe she had gotten her wish. When the front door opened, her heart leaped into her throat.

"Aren't you going to say, 'Welcome home, Trevor'?" he asked after she had stared at him for what seemed like a good five minutes. He leaned his shoulder against the doorjamb, crossing his arms over his chest. His attitude was one of eager anticipation.

She wanted to smack his cheerful grin off his face but was immediately ashamed of the impulse. It showed only the frazzled state of her nerves where the man was concerned. As Gina predicted, he had stopped calling. Just when she thought it was safe, Trevor was back.

"What are you doing here?" she managed with creditable calm, though a dreadful suspicion was lurking in the back of her mind. How did he always manage to unbalance her in just a few seconds? She could keep her temper with the surliest contractor or an indecisive client, but Trevor Planchet was a different story.

"I live here." He had the grace the look slightly contrite, and Jessie almost wished she had given in to her earlier impulse. "Don't you think you should come inside to discuss this? We don't want to disturb the neighbors when you flail me alive."

Though she was tempted to turn and walk back to her car, she nodded and walked stiffly past him into the house. Now she knew why Mrs. Langford-Hughes's offer had sounded too good to be true. In her excitement, she hadn't asked too many questions, especially after seeing the house. Looking back now, she realized that that had been extremely foolish.

"Well, how do you like it?" Trevor seemed eager to know her opinion, almost appearing nervous as he waited for her answer. He rocked back and forth on the soles of his running shoes with his hands stuffed in the pockets of his black chinos. Thankfully he was wearing a gray-and-black shirt under his vest this time.

"It's a lovely house. Did you do the renovations yourself?" She was reluctant to ask since she'd had so many complimentary thoughts about the unknown owner over the past week. The hard work and good taste that had gone into the renovations seemed at odds with the man in front of her.

"Yes. It took a couple years, but it was worth every bruised thumbnail and sore muscle." Trevor's voice was filled with well-earned pride as he absently reached up to stroke the smooth wood of the newel post. She couldn't accurately read his expression in the dim light of the brass and beveled-glass fixture overhead. "The house belonged to Daddy's aunt, but she hadn't lived here for about twenty years before she died, and it had been divided into three apartments. She asked in her will that it be taken care of properly."

"You've done an excellent job. She would have been very pleased with the way the house is coming to life again." Jessie couldn't hold back the compliment. No matter what she thought of him on a personal level, she couldn't fault his work on the old house.

"Thank you," he answered simply. He eyed her warily, almost gauging her mood before he spoke again. Lifting his hand to rub the back of his neck, he cleared his throat. Then he seemed to come to a decision. "Why don't we go into the dining room for dinner and discuss what you've been working on? Or are you considering throwing that canvas bag at me and storming out?"

She could feel herself flushing at the accuracy of his question. Just once she would like to come out the winner in an exchange with him, instead of feeling awkward and sullen. "Dinner?"

"Just a little something I had brought in," he murmured, still watching her every move.

Jessie didn't answer immediately, debating her next move. This commission was a dream of a lifetime, and she'd put too much work into it already to toss it away in a fit of pique. He wasn't going to have the satisfaction of seeing Jessie DeLord run, but she was going to stay on her terms.

"I'll stay for dinner on certain conditions."

He straightened from his relaxed poise against the banister, unconsciously reaching up to rub the slight crook in his nose. "And they are?"

"This is strictly a business arrangement, even if you did trick me into accepting the job," she stated matter-of-factly, allowing herself a tiny smile of satisfaction. Finally she was calling the shots where Trevor was concerned, and she liked it. "As soon as this turns personal, we call the whole thing off and you find another decorator."

If she didn't know better, she would think he was hurt by her requirements. That was impossible, she knew, for someone with Trevor's ego. He caught her by surprise when he said, "That sounds fair."

As she followed him through the dark shadows of the living room toward the dining room, Jessie wasn't sure that she'd done the right thing. The echoes of their footsteps on the wood flooring ominously reminded her that they were all alone. For a minute she seemed to have finally gotten the upper hand, or had she? Could she have just played into his hands? Knowing it was dangerous to continue that train of thought, she decided to wait and analyze the evening after it was over. She needed to keep her full attention on a smooth operator like Trevor Planchet.

"This is 'just a little something'?" Looking down at the linen tablecloth spread on the floor, Jessie wondered if he was planning on inviting the entire neighborhood. The cloth seemed to be covered with chafing dishes. The mingling of a number of tantalizing aromas filled her head.

"You remember my sister Tory? She owns Bill of Fare catering where Abby Bush works. Whenever I don't want to give someone ptomaine from cooking, I give them a call."

" 'The bachelor's friend,' " she murmured, remembering one of the catering firm's advertising slogans.

"That was my idea, since I was always pestering her for special meals when I— Why don't you make yourself comfortable while I get the rolls out of the oven." He swiftly headed for the kitchen, as if he wanted to be out of sight before she could ask another question.

So Trevor used his sister's cooking to help him with his conquests. Well, not tonight, she determined with a grimace as she dropped her tote bag beneath the bay window at the far end of the room. What exactly had she gotten into by agreeing to stay? Could she suggest they turn on more lights than just the chandelier with its electric bulbs that resembled flickering candles? If she had any sense, she could leave before he came back. Wrapping her arms around her waist, she wondered why the house hadn't seemed this empty or intimidating when she was here with Gina.

"Here we go."

Jessie jumped at the sound of his cheerful voice behind her. Her nerves definitely were not going to survive the evening, she decided, waiting for him to place the basket on the tablecloth. Absently she reached to run her hand over her French plait, smoothing imaginary stray hairs into place.

"Well, I guess we're ready to dig in," he stated, rubbing his hands together. "Which corner do you want to sit on?"

"Right here is fine." She sank to the floor, thankful for her turquoise divided skirt and print over-blouse that allowed her to move gracefully and modestly. By precisely arranging her skirt around her knees she didn't have to look directly at Trevor for the next few minutes, overcome with the feelings of being a shy fifteen-year-old again.

"Now, what can I tempt madam's palate with this evening? Some herb chicken or perhaps beef Burgundy?" Trevor intoned in a nasal impersonation of a five-star restaurant's maître d', a towel draped over his forearm. Scrambling around on his knees, he uncovered each dish for her inspection. "Or would madam care to partake of the shrimp Creole?"

She found herself laughing in spite of herself at his autocratic parody. Perhaps she could make it through dinner if she just relaxed and didn't look for hidden meanings. The earlier tension between them seemed to have dissipated since his return from the kitchen. "Were you preparing for an invasion?"

"I wasn't sure what you liked, so I decided on one from column A, etc.," he explained easily, moving toward another covered dish. "Voila! Mixed vegetables."

"Everything looks delicious, and I skipped lunch today. Just give me a sample of each." She realized that she was famished, and not just from sparring with

Trevor. Accepting her plate, she eagerly took her first bite. The chicken was ambrosia, and she closed her eyes to savor the explosion of spices on her tongue.

After that, there was little time for conversation as they took turns critiquing every dish like two greedy children. Jessie claimed her enthusiasm stemmed from eating microwave entrées all week, and Trevor blamed the stadium food he thrived on while in Washington. Finally, as they put down their plates, they both gave credit to the chef.

"Let me get dessert, and you can show me what you've been doing while I was out of town." In one swift movement, Trevor was on his feet. He retrieved her tote bag and placed it by her side before collecting the dirty dishes.

Jessie slowly wiped her hands on her napkin, glad for something to do while he hovered over her. For the past half hour she'd forgotten about why she was there and how it had been arranged. She couldn't let her guard down again. A charming smile and amusing conversation were the first steps to heartache, she lectured herself. Grabbing her tote bag as if it was a life line, she began to pull out her sketches and material samples.

"Say, you've been busy," Trevor said easily, placing a tempting confection of emerald green and white in front of her. "Just let me get the rest of this out of the way, and you'll have my undivided attention."

"That's exactly what I'm afraid of," Jessie murmured, staring at the parfait glass without really seeing it. She didn't know if she was going to be able to take another bite. Her palms were beginning to sweat and her pulse rate was rapidly increasing. She remembered the feeling from her first presentation in college, when her mind had gone totally blank. This time she wasn't nervous about what she had created, but about her audience.

"Okay, now let's see what you have in mind."

Jessie swallowed deeply as Trevor sprawled on the floor beside her, propping himself up on his elbow just inches from her knees. Until now he had kept his distance on the other side of the tablecloth, remaining impersonal throughout dinner as promised. With him so close, she knew that she was going to do something foolish. So she opened her mouth and began to talk about colors, textures, and contrast, anything to keep from watching Trevor as he spooned the creamy parfait into his mouth.

"No, no royal blue. I had to sleep under a velvet-blue canopy when I was growing up, and I don't ever want to do it again," he said decisively a few minutes later.

Jessie immediately began searching frantically in her bag, with no idea of what she was looking for. The image of him lying in bed had come too quickly to mind, and in her imagination, he hadn't been a little boy. It really didn't matter if he slept in the nude or not; her only interest was the bed itself and the color scheme. Was it her imagination or had he moved closer while looking over her sketches?

"I like the idea of using a combination of styles throughout the house," Trevor continued, unconscious of Jessie's dilemma. "Daddy went a little overboard at the old homestead, especially with some of the massive pieces. I do have some good pieces that Aunt Beth left. They aren't overly ornate, thank heaven. They're stored in the garage. Let's see, there's a sideboard and dining room table as well as a sofa, some chairs, a washstand with all the pitchers. Oh, and two bedsteads. Too bad Tory commandeered all the Duncan Phyfe for her cottage."

"How do you feel about a grandfather clock?" Jessie quickly grasped at the first piece of furniture she could think of, one that didn't go in a bedroom. "I thought one would look ideal in the entry hall near the staircase. It would draw the visitors' eyes to the carvings on the banister and the ceiling plasterwork."

"Terrific. Just let me know when you want to go shopping. My only limitation is nothing too heavy or ornate. We don't have to stay too true to the period. I don't want to live in a museum."

Though the look in his eyes was perfectly innocent, Jessie's breath caught in her throat for a second. "Y-you want to go shopping with me?"

"Naturally I want to go along. Why should you have all the fun?" He looked startled that she'd even question his participation. "I'm usually free until early afternoon, so we could work around your schedule."

Who wouldn't want to help pick out their own furniture, you imbecile? When in doubt, avoid the issue, she decided, beginning to put her materials in her tote bag. "That really isn't a consideration yet, so we can discuss it when I'm ready to do the furniture. I'll see if any estate sales or auctions are scheduled in the next week or so. So, is royal blue the only color you don't want?"

"I'm rather partial to turquoise and red," he murmured, spooning more ice cream into his mouth and, as he licked his lower lip, looking pointedly to where the hem of her skirt skimmed her knees.

She didn't bother to acknowledge that she understood what he was talking about, trying to resist the urge to pull her skirt down to her ankles. It was time for her to make a hasty retreat. She was sure now that he had moved closer. "Well, that should cover everything for now—"

"You haven't touched your parfait. I made that myself. You do like crème de menthe and ice cream?"

Why had her mother taught her such good manners?

She had been told to be courteous at all times. There wasn't any way she could leave without tasting the parfait and not be ashamed of herself. Reluctantly she picked up the glass and dipped in her spoon for one polite bite. The ice cream had begun to melt, but the creamy mint flavor was delicious.

"Jessie, are you really angry with me for tricking you about the house? Is it really so terrible to work for me?"

His question took her by surprise, especially since he was running his forefinger in a lazy circle over her kneecap. She was trapped where she was. The only alternative was to scramble backward in a crab-style walk, and she refused to look so foolish. She took another bite of ice cream in hopes of lowering her skyrocketing body temperature. It didn't help.

"I really couldn't think of another way to approach you," he continued, his hooded gaze masking his expression. He seemed intent on creating a pattern on her leg that seemed to be moving higher each second. Did he purposely let that shock of brown hair fall over his forehead, tempting her fingers to smooth it back in place?

Was dignity really all that important? Jessie wondered wildly, closing her free hand into a fist around her spoon.

"I think we'll have a good *partnership*, an outstanding team."

Was it the way he said *partnership* or the triumphant gleam in his eyes when he looked up suddenly that broke the spell? Jessie wasn't sure, but she knew that she was being stupid to even listen to him. She did what any self-respecting woman would do to protect herself. She dumped her parfait directly on top of his head.

While he was sputtering and wiping the gooey mess

out of his eyes, she scrambled to her feet. "That's how I feel about your juvenile deception. Much as I love this house, I'm not sure I can stand being in your company to do it," she spat out, giving her irritation at him and herself free rein. "You may think you're God's gift to women, but you're the last man I would want for a husband and to father my baby. You're an irresponsible child yourself, so how could you be expected to raise one?"

With that, she spun on her heel and stalked out of the house. A small smile of accomplishment curved her lips over the memory of Trevor's stunned look. It was apparent he'd gotten his way much too often with the female population.

The horror of what she had done didn't hit her until she was strapping on her seat belt. But she didn't regret it. In fact, when she visualized the look on Gina's face tomorrow when she told her, she began to giggle helplessly. Ten minutes later, as she wiped the tears from her eyes, Jessie put the car in gear. This was undoubtedly the last time she would see Trevor Planchet.

"What? No more sage advice on how to handle the delicate Southern woman?"

Trevor could feel the heat beginning around the rim of his ears at Logan Herrington's question late the next morning as they drove away from the Planchet house. The other man's words drowned out Garth Brooks crooning "Shameless" and reminded him of his authoritative advice on how to handle women a few weeks ago.

"I figured you've had plenty of practice by now. Of course, my sister isn't exactly typical," Trevor answered, not really sure about his views on any type of women this morning. Resisting the urge to check behind his ears for traces of crème de menthe, he waited for the northerner's response.

"I decided that your sister is probably the most stubborn, confusing woman I've ever met." The older man didn't seem to be too perturbed by the discovery.

"I should introduce you to the queen of confusion."

"Pardon?"

Trevor hadn't realized he'd spoken out loud. It just showed how turned around he felt since meeting Jessie DeLord. He always thought he understood women as well as truly appreciated them. As a mature man of thirty-five, he genuinely enjoyed the company of women as friends as well as lovers. Women were the delight of his life, until recently. For the first time, he had some sympathy for his sister's obnoxious ex-fiancé the night Tory poured a pitcher of beer over his head. The only saving grace about last night had been that there were no witnesses.

"We don't have to go buy my computer today if you don't feel up to it."

"I feel fine, Logan. I just have a problem that needs to be worked out," Trevor explained with more confidence than he felt.

"It wouldn't have anything to do with the raven-haired beauty you attacked at the Bushes' party, would it?"

Trevor glanced at the craggy features of his companion and grimaced at the laughter he saw lurking in his eyes. "Was that a lucky guess, Yankee, or has my sister been squealing on me?"

"Your father, actually. He was asking me about what happened at the Bushes' party and gave a fairly accurate description of a young woman I saw hiding from you behind a fig tree. That woman apparently bears a striking resemblance to his new decorator."

"You mean she was behind me when I was talking

to you?'' He practically groaned the question, slamming his hand against the steering wheel. Was it any wonder Jessie thought he was a jerk?

"Hey, don't abuse this car. Remember, it's a classic,'' Logan remarked, the thread of humor still in his voice. "So you're having trouble with this—now how was it you put it?—this delicate flower who has to be gently nurtured.''

"This one usually has the manners of an angel, but I discovered last night that she also has a temper that makes my sister look downright placid,'' Trevor grumbled, rubbing the crook of his nose where his sister had accidently broken it when he was ten.

"Does she have a name?''

"Jessica DeLord, and she thinks I'm pond scum right now,'' he informed the other man as he pulled into a parking place in front of the computer store. "In fact, I'm not fit to father her baby.'' He climbed out of the car in jerky movements as he, yet again, relived the most humiliating moment of his life.

"You *are* a fast worker.''

"Not that fast,'' Trevor returned wryly, pulling open the glass door to the store. "We've only had one lunch and a dinner together. I don't know how we managed to fast-forward into marriage, much less curtain climbers. I'm trying not to think about that. It's not that I don't like kids, but right now my main concern is damage control. She was going to decorate my house.''

" 'Was'?'' Logan didn't mask his interest, barely looking at the selection of portable computers on display around them.

"She's damn good, too. You should have seen the ideas that she'd come up with in a week, but—'' He broke off, at a loss of how to explain what had happened without embarrassing himself any further.

"But you really wouldn't care if she was color-blind," Logan diplomatically finished for him.

"Exactly," Trevor answered, giving his companion an appreciative smile. His confidence was beginning to return now that he had a sympathetic ear. There was nothing better than discussing the matter with another man to restore a guy's equilibrium. "This thing about babies has me baffled; however, that isn't my biggest problem right now. Everything else is academic until I can get her to speak to me again. On top of everything else, we have that damn car rally this weekend."

"Flowers, candy, or jewelry?"

"Hey, I don't know why they say Yankees can't be romantic," Trevor exclaimed. Logan's words had triggered an inspiration. It certainly couldn't put him in the dog house any further. How could she refuse a humble, sincere apology? He would be out of sight for the next three days while her temper cooled down. It was perfect.

"Are you sure this baby thing isn't a problem yet?" A frown of concern creased Logan's forehead.

"The only problem is why I don't find the prospect so horrifying. If any other woman I know mentioned the *B* word, I would have run screaming in the other direction," Trevor admitted a little sheepishly. He'd lain awake last night thinking about a miniature version of Jessie. It was incredible and yet terrifying. He also knew the idea was ridiculous to contemplate at this juncture of their relationship, if that's what it could be called.

Right now he had to get within at least shouting distance of the lady. He could hire another decorator, but he didn't want to replace Jessie in his life until he could figure out why she had him so preoccupied. She might think he was on her reject list, but he was going to change her mind. All he had to do was figure out what he'd done wrong so far. As he quickly reviewed the past few weeks, he shuddered. What had he done right?

FIVE

"Excuse me, I'm looking for Jessica DeLord."

At the sound of her name, Jessie turned away from unlocking the door of Aesthetics, Ltd. A young woman stood before her carrying a large box sprouting balloons from a hole in the top. "That's me. Would you wait a minute while I unlock the door?"

Jessie had just returned from an afternoon meeting with Grisham and Collins at the Planchet building. Within a matter of minutes, she had the door open, the answering machine switched off, and had instructed the delivery person to place the box on the closest flat surface. After absentmindedly tipping the young woman, Jessie simply stared at the package, almost afraid to open it. With Gina gone for a doctor's appointment, she was tempted to toss out the box before her partner returned. She could think of only one person who would think to send balloons.

"Let's see, they run water on packages that are suspected to carry explosives, don't they?" she murmured, moving to view the box from the other side as if it might be an incendiary device. After another two minutes of indecision, she gave up. "Don't be such a wee-nie, DeLord."

"Hey, you got me a present and you haven't even heard my news yet." Gina's voice rang out just as Jessie pulled a familiar item from the box. "Then again, maybe you didn't. Isn't that your tote bag?"

"Yes, it is. I left it at the Dalrymple house last night." Why did Trevor do these things to her? Until a few weeks ago, her life had been so sane, so normal.

"How come I feel like I came in during the middle of the movie?"

One look at Gina's hands-on-hip pose told Jessie she was going to have trouble, again. Jessie hadn't quite gotten around to telling her partner the identity of the homeowner and had thought she might in another month or two. Maybe it would be much simpler to tell her about Trevor this morning.

"Aren't you going to see what else is in the box?" Gina asked.

"What else?" Already composing her explanation about last night, Jessie had forgotten about the package.

"Those balloons are being anchored by something." Gina nodded her head toward the miniature silver dirigibles that had multicolored expressions of remorse written across their surfaces.

What could he have sent besides her tote bag? Jessie tilted the box cautiously to the side and peeked inside. A plush blue-and-white lop-eared rabbit was peering up at her over the rim of black plastic glasses. The balloons were securely held in one paw, an envelope filling the other. She grabbed the rodent by its chubby waist and let the box slide to the floor. The three-foot rabbit sat on the table, resplendent in his white vest and pocket watch.

"He's adorable. So why did Trevor send him?"

"How did you know who sent it?" Jessie asked without thinking, and bit her lip in vexation as Gina rolled her eyes. Instead of saying anything else incriminating, she tore open the envelope. The distinctive masculine scrawl asked her to forgive him for his clumsiness and his subterfuge in getting her to decorate the house. Two entire paragraphs praised her talents, then he humbly asked her to continue working on the house. He would live up to the agreement, if that was what it took to keep her on the job.

"What agreement? Jesssieeeeee." Gina drew out her friend's name to show the level of her frustration at being left in the dark. She didn't bother to look guilty about reading over her partner's shoulder. "Does this mean Trevor Planchet owns the Dalrymple house? The man is a true romantic."

" 'Romantic'? You call lying and scheming romantic?" She shook her head in dismay but couldn't keep from running her forefinger down one of the rabbit's fuzzy ears. Just as Trevor had intended, she had a clear memory of the night they met. The man definitely had his own unique style, she admitted reluctantly; however, that was something she was going to keep to herself.

"Lying and scheming can be romantic when there's a good motive," Gina asserted before picking up the rabbit and depositing him squarely on Jessie's desk. "The man is obviously smitten."

" 'Smitten'? Are you getting enough oxygen to your brain?"

"Okay. He has the hots for you, and you're a fool if you don't give him a chance to prove that he isn't the louse you imagine." She turned to Jessie, her expression grim. "If you don't promise to give Trevor Planchet one more chance, I'm not going to let you be the godmother to my child. I need someone with brains for that job."

"Gina, this really— Godmother? What are you talking about?"

"My doctor's appointment and the indigestion I've been having lately," she explained simply, a smile blossoming across her face. Almost on reflex, her hand covered her stomach. "I'm pregnant a year ahead of schedule, and it's all your fault."

"I don't think I had anything to do with this," Jessie returned, but ruined her perplexed look by hugging her friend. Pulling away, she said very seriously, "I think Jeff is the one to blame."

"He isn't the one who started talking about babies nonstop three months ago." Gina leaned her hip against the desk and crossed her arms over her chest, her schoolmarm look firmly in place. "You were the one who pointed out that there was an epidemic of pregnancy among our friends. That was what set off this idea that you wanted to have a baby before it was too late, which led to the insane plans of yours to find the perfect husband to be the father."

"Well, we did go to five baby showers in a row, and all the prospective mothers were over thirty," Jessie admitted. "You, however, were the one who saw the talk show about older women having babies and the two women who decided they should go for the whole works—career, husband, and a baby. You even bragged that you had four more years before the panic age of forty."

"I thought it was incredible that anyone would go to those lengths, especially women who are old enough to know better. You weren't supposed to take it so seriously." Gina's accusing look made Jessie shift her feet from side to side uneasily. "The next thing I knew, you were hip deep in those silly books on pregnancy for older women and dating in the nineties. So, it *is* your fault. I got pregnant by osmosis.'' Gina smiled in triumph at her brilliant theory.

"I give up.'' Jessie threw her hands up in a show of surrender. Her partner was one of the most difficult people to argue with once she got an idea into her head. Maybe a nice cup of tea would get them settled for the rest of the afternoon, Jessie decided as she walked toward the credenza.

"And?''

The single word stopped Jessie halfway to her destination. She glanced over her shoulder to inquire, "And what?''

"You're going to give Trevor a chance to make amends by continuing to work on the Dalrymple house.''

Jessie turned to face her friend; however, her glance fell on the blue-and-white rabbit first. If Trevor kept to her rules, there really wouldn't be a problem. It was a big if, she knew. Or was it wishful thinking on her part that he wouldn't? her traitorous little inner voice asked. Unwilling to consider the matter, she looked at her partner's belligerent expression. "All right, I will work on the Dalrymple house. That's all I'm going to promise.''

There was a lengthy silence as the two women regarded each other, each almost challenging the other to relent. Gina gave in first. "Well, it's a start,'' she said grudgingly before heading toward her own desk. "But don't think I'm not going to check up on how you're treating the poor man. I'm griping for two now.''

Poor man, my foot. Jessie almost said the words out loud, gazing at the innocent rabbit on the desk. Inwardly she sighed over her friend's lack of sympathy. How was she going to hold out against a rogue like Trevor Planchet without an ally? She couldn't protect herself against his practiced assaults if no one was going to come to her defense. Unfortunately, she seemed to be weakening.

Pouring herself a hot cup of tea, she wondered if her mother had felt the same way all those years ago. Was that why she let her father hurt her over and over again until the final separation, because she couldn't stay angry at her husband? A shiver skated down Jessie's spine, and she knew that it was an omen of dangerous times again. Her emotions were already in a chaotic state, and the man had sent her only a silly rabbit.

At least Gina hadn't asked for any details about last night, so her juvenile behavior was still a secret.

Trevor stood on the doorstep at nine o'clock, wondering what he was doing. When he'd left the rally planning meeting at Curtiss's, his car seemed to have had a mind of its own. Since he had a few days off due to the car rally, he could have stayed with the others for a relaxing evening. At their protests, he told his friends that he wanted to turn in early for a change and be fresh for the rally weekend.

So why was he standing on Jessie's doorstep? Was that what Logan's cryptic thumbs-up signal had meant before he left the house? Had the other man known what he was going to do before Trevor himself? It really didn't matter. He was here now, so he had to do something about it.

Before he could reconsider, he pressed his thumb to the doorbell. She couldn't think he was any more of an idiot than she did already. So why did he have the urge to run when he didn't hear any sounds from behind the door?

Time seemed to stand still. He knew she had enough time to reach the door and check through the peep hole; in fact, he stood back so she would have a clear view. Still, the door didn't open. Just as he was about to give up hope, the porch light went on. A second later he heard the bolt turn and the door began to inch open.

"Hello." That was all he could manage at the surprising sight of Jessie dressed in baggy brilliant-orange sweats. Damn, she looked like a blue blood even in misshapen clothes and a ponytail. His taut muscles relaxed. She was alone. Without realizing it, he'd been wondering if she might have had company, of the male variety.

"Trevor." Her husky voice washed over him, soothing his erratic nerves. She didn't sound surprised or angry. He hoped he didn't do anything inadvertently to change that.

"I was on the way home from a meeting at my brother's house out on Highway Ten and thought I'd stop in to get your answer in person." *Why not tell her everything you did today?* he chided himself.

She didn't bother to question what answer he wanted. He held his breath when she hesitated a moment before saying, "Won't you come in? It's a little chilly to stand here talking."

He nodded and silently stepped inside. Was it his imagination, or did she seem much more at ease in his company tonight? Of course, he hadn't done anything stupid yet. Was she being nice because tonight was the end of their brief acquaintance? he wondered as he followed her into the living room.

"Please sit down. Would you like something to drink?" she asked politely as if she were entertaining the minister.

"No, thank you," he returned in the same civil tone. He took a seat on the edge of a horsehair chair, feeling as stiff as any of his Victorian ancestors. Not wanting to make a false move, he waited for Jessie to speak. She moved quickly around the room, turning on two more lamps. Her glance strayed more than once to the table near his elbow.

"I want to thank you for the rabbit and the balloons," she stated, her hands clasped primly in front of her. Standing in the middle of the room, she had the stance of the perfect society hostess. "I really think I owe you an apology as well. There was no excuse for what I did. I overreacted, and I'm sorry."

Should he accept her apology? Would he be damned if he did, or damned if he didn't? Maybe he should simply be noncommittal. "That's all right."

Silence descended again, making Trevor look around for anything that would be a suitable topic. Jessie's fondness for Victorian decor showed clearly in her choices. The medallion-backed sofa and parlor chairs were good reproductions, much more delicate than the furniture he'd grown up around. The fringed shaded lamps and other bric-a-brac were antiques that blended well with more contemporary pieces. On the marble-topped table next to him were a number of photographs in ornate frames, almost hidden by a pile of books. He cursorily glanced at the titles, then reached over to pick up a photograph of a large group of people.

"Is this your family?" He glanced up to find her brilliant blue gaze trained on him. Her expression was hard to read, almost bittersweet.

"Yes, those are my brothers and sisters on the farm in Tennessee."

"You've come a long way from a Tennessee farm." He was impressed with what she had accomplished.

"Hearing my life story wasn't why you came here tonight, though," she answered quickly, seeming to shake off the memory conjured up by his question about her family.

Realizing that she didn't want to say any more about her family, he took a deep breath. He might as well get this over with as quickly and as painlessly as possible. "No, I came to find out if you're still going to work on my house."

"Yes."

He cocked his head to the side, waiting to see if there was more. "Yes, that's all?"

Jessie actually smiled, sending his pulse rate into double time. There was some quality he still couldn't quite define when she smiled. He wished he could pin it down. That might be the answer to his fascination with the lady. Maybe it was only because he hadn't seen her smile at him very often.

"I'll reserve judgment for now," she answered easily, her expression almost turning playful. "My partner says I haven't been very fair to you. So I will try to keep an open mind, within reason."

He smiled grudgingly in return. Who had been treating whom unfairly? Tonight was going to be a sleepless night over Jessie again, he acknowledged glumly. She was one surprise after another. He had been sure she would turn him down; that was why he hadn't waited until Monday to see her. The suspense had been gnawing at him. Maybe he should also send her friend a token of appreciation for her defense of him. He was probably going to need all the help he could get. Unable to think of another topic to discuss, he rose to his feet to leave.

The lady hadn't expected his sudden movement and took a cautious step backward. He smiled sadly at her reaction. "I'm not really all that dangerous."

Jessie didn't answer, merely raising an arched brow that seemed to contradict his words. He simply walked to the front door, trying to tamp down his instincts. What he wanted most in the world at that moment was to take Jessie in his arms. He was sure, however, that would be the worst move he could make. She remained silent as she followed him to the door.

When he grasped the doorknob, he turned to glance down at her. For perhaps the first time, she wasn't looking at him with anger or disdain. Her blue eyes were wide with curiosity. Even without make-up, her face was alluring.

Not stopping to think about his actions, not calculating the result, he slowly bent his head. His lips feathered across the full warmth of hers. Reluctantly, he raised his head. She didn't pull away, which he thought was encouraging. The temptation of her flushed face and slumberous eyes was too great, and he bent to kiss her again.

Just as before, the world went into a tailspin. A mixture of feelings coursed through him. He felt a basic, primitive desire for the soft woman in his arms, mingled with a need to cherish and protect her. When she trembled against him, his arms tightened instinctively, but he didn't deepen the kiss. He didn't trust himself.

"I'm not dangerous," he told her, his voice not quite steady, "but I don't have much will power where you're concerned. I'll try to keep to the agreement, but I won't promise that I'll always keep my hands to myself."

Before she could say a word, he walked out the door, closing it firmly behind him. Pausing on the front step, he took a deep breath to clear his head. Even a brief kiss from Jessie was potent. He had felt her lips move under his, he was sure of it. Liquid desire still coursed through him, and he wondered if he would be able to survive actually making love with her.

As he ambled to his car, a sudden thought occurred to him. What was a woman like Jessica DeLord doing with books on dating and babies? More important, what was Jessie's preoccupation with babies? Before he grasped the door handle he looked back at the house. He tried to remember the titles of the books by the photographs. Shaking his head, he climbed into the car. Every time he solved one piece of the puzzle about the lady, another one seemed to spring up.

"Hi, beautiful."

Jessie almost spilled her tea on the fabric samples in front of her. Somehow Trevor had materialized out of nowhere after a three-day absence and was now sitting on the edge of her desk. "Hello."

"Did you miss me over the weekend?"

She caught the teasing glint in his brown eyes and relaxed. After Thursday night, she decided to take things one day at a time. She wasn't going to let Trevor goad her into any rash behavior. They'd been able to have a rational conversation that night, so if she was careful, they could get along. She just refused to remember his departure. "Was I supposed to miss you?"

"You could pretend. At least tell me that the news was flat without me."

"I don't watch the local news." She smiled gently to soften her denial. As long as she kept her distance from him and didn't think about her physical reaction to his touch, she was perfectly all right. At least she was with the width of the desk between them.

"That's sacrilege!" he exclaimed, clasping his hand to his heart in a movement that was terribly familiar to Jessie. With Trevor now attired in an old football jersey and jeans, the gesture wasn't quite as dramatic as the first time she'd seen it.

"So sue me. Did you come in here only to harass me, or was there a reason?" she asked brightly, more than pleased with her handling of the situation. Leaning back in her chair, she was able to look at Trevor and see her partner's stunned reaction to the by-play.

"A little of both, actually, as my friend Logan says. I wanted to show you these pictures of the kitchen cabinets we're putting in this week." He passed her the photographs before he continued. "We're planning to use a light walnut stain on the wood. Sometime while you're shopping around for some items, would you look for some dishes and glasses that would be displayed well in the upper cabinets?"

"I think so." Looking at the picture of the glass-fronted cabinet, she felt yet another twinge of longing to own this house. Apparently her thoughts were all too clear.

"Love my house, tolerate me?"

"That about sums up the matter."

"Jessie!" Gina's chastisement broke in before Trevor could respond. "You shouldn't be rude to a client."

"He started it," she shot back, realizing that she was enjoying herself without feeling threatened. Maybe this partnership was going to work after all. Then she looked up and was stunned at the sudden transformation in Trevor's expression.

One minute, he was boyishly teasing. A second later, after his attention strayed over her shoulder, a blatantly sensual smile curved his lips. He didn't bother to hide the masculine appreciation in his gaze as he looked down at her.

"Nice rabbit," he said only for her ears.

She could feel the heat rushing into her cheeks. Although she'd taken the deflating balloons home, the rabbit now stood next to her credenza. The beast was only there to remind her to go very carefully, not what Trevor seemed to think. The man had a distinctly proprietary air about him now.

The phone rang before she could disabuse him of the

idea. "Oh, hello, Wes. No, I can't really talk right now," she said, blessing him silently for calling at that moment. Trevor seemed to be looming closer, a frown taking the place of his seductive look. "Yes, that sounds wonderful. Why don't I meet you at the restaurant about five-thirty? Thank your client for me as well. I'm looking forward to it. Bye."

"Who's Wes? Another idiot lawyer?"

"He's an accountant," she answered, making a show of opening her organizer to write down the name and time. With an air of surprise, she looked up and asked, "Was there anything else besides the cabinets you wanted to discuss?"

"Not right now," he answered, making it clear that he still had some unfinished business to discuss. His eyes had darkened to almost black. "Just remember that I didn't make any promises."

He stood up and walked quickly to the door. Just as he was about to step into the corridor, Jessie called his name and he turned back to face her. "Don't push me, Trevor. I have my limits."

He left without another word.

"Well, that was the most disgusting performance I've ever seen," Gina exclaimed, barely waiting for the door to swing shut.

"I thought you liked Trevor." Jessie gave her friend a wide-eyed innocent look.

"Don't be obtuse. I was talking about you." Her temper was beginning to show from the rapid tapping of her pencil against her desk blotter. "I thought you were going to give Trevor a chance?"

"I said I would be nice to him. I didn't say I was going to throw myself at his feet." For a moment, she remembered a few nights earlier when she had melted against him the second he touched her. What Gina didn't know wouldn't hurt her. She had enough trouble with her friend's loyalty without admitting the man's kisses should be declared lethal weapons.

"Do you really think he fell for that 'other man' nonsense? The jealousy routine went out years ago."

"I wasn't trying to make him jealous," Jessie shot back more heatedly than she intended. "I didn't arrange for Wes to call. A grateful client gave him tickets to *Les Miz* for Thursday night. Wes usually doesn't make plans this close to the tax deadline, but he didn't want to miss this."

Gina's answer was a snort of disgust as she returned to her work. The floor plan in front of Jessie was neglected as she reviewed this last encounter with Trevor. She realized that he had changed his tactics, but just what was he going to do next?

"Tory, this wasn't quite what I had in mind when I asked you to have lunch with me," Trevor complained from his seat on the freezer in the Bill of Fare kitchen. His sister and Abby were busy shouting orders at the workmen in the front of the shop.

"I'm feeding you and not putting you to work, so stop whining," she called to him before she disappeared through the swinging red saloon doors.

He bit viciously into his sandwich to appease his feelings. Tory was preoccupied with expanding her catering business to retail stores, the first one opening in two days. If he could just get her to stand still for ten minutes, he'd get out of her way.

"You know, after that prank you and Curtiss pulled on me on Saturday night after the rally, I really shouldn't be talking to you at all," Tory snapped as she bustled back through the doorway. She propped her hips against the freezer and grabbed his hand to steal a bite of his sandwich.

"Hey, get your own, Piglet." He then regretted reverting to her childhood nickname. He wanted her to be on his side. It was just as well she didn't know about the little talk he and Curtiss had with Logan on Saturday evening over dinner. If she was annoyed that they had tricked her into driving Logan back to Little Rock from the rally, then she wouldn't be thrilled about her two brothers playing good-cop/bad-cop to find out the guy's intentions.

"So what was so all-fired important that you got out of bed at a decent hour?"

"Don't get too smart, or I'll tell the Yankee that you're madly in love with him." He couldn't help teasing her and enjoyed seeing his usually self-possessed sister blush. "I need to ask your advice about—" He broke off as Abby came through the swinging door.

"Did I come in at a bad time, I hope?" She gave Trevor a threatening look to tell him he was still in the doghouse. He groaned inwardly, since Abby was the last person he wanted to overhear this.

"I think my big brother is having girl trouble. Isn't that cute?" Tory teased, ready to get back at him, though still unaware of the worst of her family's interference in her personal life.

He debated on telling his sister about the family's betting pool on how soon she and Logan would be engaged. Looking at the sharp knife she was wielding as she prepared her sandwich, he decided against it. Besides, he owed some loyalty to Logan, even if he was a Yankee. He also had his money on a week from Wednesday and didn't want to ruin the odds.

"You might as well go ahead and spill your guts," Tory told him, jumping up beside him a few minutes later. "Abby probably isn't going to leave."

"It's not that exciting. I'm just getting some mixed signals from this particular lady," he said grudgingly as Abby wrinkled her nose at him. "I think she likes me, but I'm not sure if she'll go out with me if I ask her. I've done a couple of dumb things that involve her, so now she's a little wary of me.''

"This must be pretty important, if you're scared to approach her." His sister munched on her sandwich, her dark eyes watching his every move.

"I talked to her yesterday, so I'm not scared of her. She just confused me. She accepted a date with someone else while I was sitting right there on her desk." He couldn't hide his indignation over what had happened. "She seems to have some ideal type of man, and I apparently don't fit the bill.''

"What? She doesn't want to date some irresponsible ex-jock who has a warped sense of humor? Smart girl,'' Abby put in. "I've told you there isn't an intelligent woman in the city who will take a risk of being your next victim.''

"You make me sound like Bluebeard, for God's sake,'' he grumbled, wondering if there really was a conspiracy against him. This is what Jessie had brought him to: paranoia. "Look, I'm not sure, but I think this one could be serious. I didn't even flinch when she mentioned babies.''

That announcement left both women speechless, but not for long. Tory was the first to break the silence. "Let's back up a little bit, okay? You can't get a date with this woman, but she's been talking about having a baby. She sounds like she has her priorities a little mixed up.''

"I'm not exactly sure what the deal is about the babies. It has something to do with my not being responsible enough to father her children. She was kinda angry at the time.''

"She wouldn't be responsible for the crème de menthe stain on my linen tablecloth, would she?'' Tory's smile was pure malice as she considered the matter. "And Arnette was complaining about mysterious green stains on some of your clothes in the laundry she did this weekend. The woman didn't happen to use you for target practice, did she?"

"You don't have to look so pleased about it."

"I told you not too long ago you'd have a hard time finding a woman crazy enough to take you seriously," his sister declared, waving a pickle spear at him to emphasize her point. "What you're going to have to do is quit pulling stunts like that one at Abby's party. No woman is going to put up with your grabbing strange women and kissing them as a practical joke."

"That's true. Darn, I still haven't called Jessie to apologize to her about that," Abby added, making Trevor break out in a cold sweat. He didn't want Abby and Jessie comparing notes too soon, at least not until Jessie got to know him a little better.

"Your best bet is to show her that you can behave like a rational, adult man." Tory scrutinized him from head to toe. "That may be tough, but you might be able to pull it off. What about this guy she accepted the date with?"

"All I know about him is that he's an accountant." He shrugged as if it didn't matter, while thinking about taking a satisfying punch at the guy.

"Since she's going out with him, he must fit her scale of perfection," Tory decided after a moment's consideration. "Your next move is to find out about this list of hers, then see what the competition is like."

Trevor finished his sandwich in two bites, digesting his sister's advice as well. Jessie said that her partner told her to be nice to him. Would Gina be willing to tell him about Jessie's list of requirements for the ideal man? And maybe she knew about the baby business as well. After saying good-bye to Abby and his sister, he walked down the mall in a much better frame of mind.

The minute he was out of sight, Abby turned to her boss. "Do you think he's going to make any progress with Jessie?"

"I don't know," she answered honestly, chewing on her lower lip as she considered the matter. "You'd better lighten up on him the next time, though. He might get a little suspicious."

"I didn't do anything," the blonde exclaimed innocently.

"But you were planning to."

"All right, so I was going to introduce them at my party. As it turned out I didn't have to." She shrugged off the matter but couldn't resist giggling over the situation.

"It really is kind of funny," Tory admitted, sharing her friend's amusement, "but there will be blood on the moon if he even thought we knew about him and Jessie. He threatened me that day at the office."

"I can imagine it had something to do with a certain Yankee."

Tory's smile quickly disappeared with the allusion to Logan Herrington. "We can't stand here talking all day. There's too much to get done before the opening."

_____ **SIX** _____

Two days later, Jessie hesitated at the doorway to Trevor's bedroom, a pen and pad in her hand, listening to Restless Heart sing their signature tune through her portable radio headphones. This was the last room on her list, and the song wasn't helping her resolve. She'd already checked the other two rooms that had posed a problem, and that left her at an impasse. All she had to do before she returned to the office was to step across the threshold.

She'd been avoiding the sparsely furnished room since she discovered the identity of the owner. Knowing who slept here made her presence seem more like an invasion than simply checking measurements. For over a week she had been in and out of the house, carefully scheduling the time for when she was sure Trevor was gone, and she had been in every room except this one.

He hadn't bothered to make the huge brass bed today. The rumpled sheet and indented pillow heightened the sense of his presence, as if he was going to step from the bathroom just finished with his shower. She adjusted the volume on her headphones as Michael Bolton began a soulful ballad. Double checking the .

window measurements wasn't really that important today, was it?

Taking a step backward, she told herself the decision to wait had nothing to do with the discarded shirt at the foot of the bed. She knew she was acting like an idiot. It was only a room, nothing more. But she took another step backward only to collide with something solid. A split second later, an arm snaked around her waist. Her scream drowned out Michael Bolton's smoky voice. Then the music was gone, the earphones pulled off her head.

"Dammit, Jessie," Trevor swore in her ear, "you took about ten years off my life."

She couldn't stop trembling, leaning limply against the solid warmth of his body and gasping, "You didn't do much for my blood pressure, either."

"I'm sorry, sweetheart. I came up the back stairs and didn't know anyone was here." His left arm curled around her shoulders, enclosing her in a soothing embrace. As he rubbed his cheek against her hair, Jessie relaxed in the comfort of his arms. Tinny sounds coming from the headphones looped around his forearm, however, quickly brought her back to reality.

She reached up automatically to turn off the radio. "I didn't know you were home. I've been here for a half hour checking some measurements."

"I was out in the garage working on the kitchen cabinets and came up to get ready for work," he explained, the words warm and moist against her ear. His heartbeat was strong, slightly fast, against her back and echoing the rhythm of her own. "Do you wear this gadget often?" he asked, holding up the headphones.

"It helps me concentrate on the numbers when I'm alone." Silently, she pledged that she was never going to wear them in his house again. Now that her initial terror had dissipated, she became all too aware of the masculine body holding her in the dark hallway. There wasn't an inch to spare between her and his lean, hard body. Her difficulty in breathing seemed to be increasing, not decreasing. Staring down at the pen and pad on the floor, she wondered what to do with her hands, resisting the urge to run them over the corded arm around her waist.

"I don't think you want to move just yet." The words were clipped in response to her slight movement.

"Trevor, I can't stand here all day." Desperation made her impatient. All she wanted to do was give in to temptation and rest her head in the hollow of his shoulder.

"I'm not dressed, Jessie."

Immediately, she froze in place. "What are you saying?"

"I don't have on any clothes."

She wasn't sure why he sounded exasperated about the situation, but her mind wasn't functioning very well. "Why?"

"Why what?"

"Why don't you have on any clothes?" she snapped, suddenly very conscious of the thin material of her silky print dress. Her back felt like it was on fire, and she didn't want to think about the other sensations she was feeling. She shifted her feet, hoping to put some distance between them.

"Don't wiggle." His curt words shot through her like an electric shock. "I had a towel, but I think it's on the floor now. It wasn't a very big towel anyway, just a courtesy to any curious neighbors while I sprinted up the stairs."

"Are you making any sense?" she asked wildly, not really listening to him. She was concentrating with great difficulty on not thinking about his body, or hers.

"Yes, I think so." His voice sounded rough to her

ears, and confused. "My clothes were pretty grimy when I came in, and I used the sauna to loosen up my muscles. I didn't check for towels until I got out and could only find a kitchen towel. The only windows with curtains are in the kitchen and my bedroom. Now do you understand?"

His warm breath tickled her neck, and she tried not to shiver in response. "W—what do you suggest we do?"

"Damned if I know."

"Trevor."

"Look, I'm trying to be a gentleman about this, but it's getting damned ha— difficult. I'm not made of stone."

Neither am I. She closed her eyes and immediately regretted it. A clear vision of his taut, muscular body materialized, one she'd been trying to suppress just minutes earlier while staring at his bed. The sound of their erratic breathing echoed in the ominously silent hallway.

"Okay, this is what we're going to do," he announced abruptly, making her start in reaction to the sudden sound. Trevor groaned. "You're going to close your eyes very tightly so I can disappear with some dignity into the bedroom. Okay? And for my sake, don't nod."

"Yes, I understand." And she did, more than he knew. She wasn't sure she would be able to stand alone if he let go of her, but she couldn't tell him that. He couldn't know that her body was melting from the inside, all her senses centered on the rigid pressure against her buttocks.

"Okay, sweetheart, close your eyes and no peeking."

Jessie didn't bother to answer his attempt at humor. She was too preoccupied for bracing herself for the moment he would release her, hoping she wouldn't collapse at his feet. With her eyes closed, the minutes passed like hours. Then she realized he was still holding her. "Trevor?"

He didn't answer immediately, his arms at her waist and shoulders tightening slightly. His mouth was warm and moist against her ear and the tender skin of her neck, making her lightheaded. "I want you to remember that I was a gentleman about this, Jessica DeLord, and someday soon, the sooner the better, I'm going to claim my reward."

Suddenly she was free. Jessie didn't look back, scrambling down the stairway as fast as she could the minute the bedroom door closed. When she reached the bottom, she sagged against the banister. She had just experienced the most harrowing twenty minutes of her life. Though she wasn't an innocent, those minutes in Trevor's arms were more intoxicating than any intimacy she'd shared with another man. If she hadn't suspected that he was a dangerous man before this, she knew it now.

Until today, she was sure she could withstand any of his snares. All he had done was hold her. She would have been putty in his hands if he had decided to press his advantage. It wasn't fair that she was falling under the spell of an irresponsible man. Hadn't her father's betrayal of her mother taught her a harsh enough lesson?

Looking toward the top of the stairs, she knew that she was going to have to face her demon soon. Avoiding Trevor wasn't doing any good. In fact, she wondered if delaying the inevitable wasn't heightening her sense of jeopardy. Dragging a hand through her tousled hair, she knew she wasn't in any condition to make a decision right now. In her weakened state of mind, it made perfect sense to climb the stairs and join Trevor in the shower.

She resolutely stood up straight and slowly walked to the door. The first move would have to come from him. He'd been dropping by the office each day, his conversation teasing and sensual, but he hadn't so much as suggested a lunch date. What exactly did he want from her? Her conditions for working on the house echoed in her mind. Since when had Trevor paid attention to anything she said?

"How are things on the baby front?"

Trevor glared across the table at Logan. "If you knew what I went through just a couple of hours ago, you wouldn't be smiling."

The other man relaxed against the wooden back of the booth. "Is that why you're drinking three hours before air time?"

"I did the early report tonight." Trevor took a swig from the long-necked bottle but didn't really taste the beer. His mind was still returning to the agonizing moments in the hallway. Life just wasn't fair, he decided. "You know, for years I've been fairly happy, having a good time with my life. Now I'm beginning to wonder if I'm being punished for having a good time."

"It can't be all that bad."

"Have you ever had to work at being a gentleman in a situation that was downright explosive?" he asked earnestly.

"Do you really want me to answer that with your sister trying to teach me how to be a Southern gentleman over the past few weeks?"

Trevor considered the matter and decided that it wouldn't be a good idea to ask too many probing questions. Like any rational man, he didn't want to know what was happening in his sister's love life. He was satisfied with the interrogation he and Curtiss had held a few days earlier. "You can't be doing any worse than

I am. I keep trying to show her that I'm just an average guy, but somehow I keep making matters worse. That's where this retribution thing for my past sins comes in. By now Jessie either thinks I'm an idiot or a sex maniac.''

"Why not simply sit down and talk to her about the problem?''

"That's reasonable, except I can't quite get up the nerve,'' Trevor answered, grimacing over the admission. "Ain't that downright macho? I think I'm not facing the problem because I don't want her to disappear out of my life just yet. If she can't reject me, I still have a chance. That's why I haven't followed Tory's advice yet.''

"What advice is Tory giving out?'' Logan sat forward, his eyes glittering with interest.

"Think it might give you some insight into my sister's tortuous brain? Well, she said I needed to find out what qualities Jessie is looking for in a man, since I know I'm not a shining example.'' He waited for Logan's comment, then continued when the other man remained silent. "I've considered calling her partner. Gina seems to be on my side and might be able to fill me in on my shortcomings.''

"Not a bad idea, unless you think your Jessie might resent this little conspiracy later.''

"That's a possibility, but in this case I think the end justifies the means,'' Trevor rationalized, suddenly feeling a weight lift off his shoulders. "Naturally, there's always the chance the list of my faults might be insurmountable.''

"She's that important to you, then?'' Logan sent Trevor a compassionate look, showing his friend that he understood his dilemma.

"I think so. At least she's too important to let go before I figure out how I feel,'' he responded, still not quite ready to surrender his freedom. Though he'd let desire overcome his common sense a few times in his checkered past, he was discovering that dealing with deeper emotions was a much more thought-provoking and intimidating prospect.

"Being serious about a particular woman isn't a fate worse than death, you know," his companion informed him with a rueful smile. "All you have to do is convince her of the same thing."

"Now we're back to my original problem. She made conditions when she agreed to keep working on my house. No monkey business, or she walks." Trevor curled his lip and took another swig of beer. Women simply didn't play fair, he determined in his irritation.

"Have you kept to the agreement?"

"More or less."

"How has she reacted?"

He thought for a moment, and a smile replaced his scowl. "She hasn't quit." Then he remembered that afternoon. "Today may have done it, even if it wasn't my fault."

"I think you need to see how she really feels about those conditions. Women have been known to say one thing but mean another," Logan informed him earnestly. "I think they have as much trouble surrendering to the inevitable as we do. Sometimes I think they're testing us, not realizing that they hold all the power in this game."

"I've tried making her mad, and that fell flat. I think I came off as a fractious juvenile trying to capture her attention."

"Maybe you should challenge her instead of making her angry. I think that's how your sister caught me." With that cryptic comment, he signaled the waiter hovering near the bar. "I felt I had to prove she was wrong."

"Challenge her." Trevor considered the matter. By trying to make Jessie angry he'd pushed her too far, pressured her into striking back at him. A challenge would appeal to her sense of fair play. Did women understand that principle, or was it simply a masculine prerogative?

"That way she might even think she's in control," Logan added. "It becomes a matter of pride. Now, I think it's time for some coffee, don't you?"

"Sure, sure." He was positive Logan was on to something. Pride was the key, something he understood all too well after the past few weeks. That old quote about pride teased the back of his mind. How much did Jessie's pride have to do with her refusal to become involved with him? He remembered that day at lunch. She had become extremely regal, almost affronted, when he had said she didn't have to be afraid to go out with him. Was her pride holding her other emotions in check?

"Hey, are you still with me?"

Trevor blinked and focused on the man across from him. "You know, it might not be so bad having a Yankee for a brother-in-law, after all."

"Let's not get too far ahead of ourselves," Logan cautioned, though a smile softened his angular features as he leaned back to allow the waiter to set down two mugs of coffee. "Jessie and Tory sound like they have a lot in common when it comes to stubbornness and pride."

"But a man born and bred in Boston wouldn't know anything about pride." Trevor couldn't resist the jab now that he was feeling more in control. He would give Jessie a few days to regroup, then he was going to begin chipping away at her defenses in earnest. The fascination that began the night he met her had turned to a hunger that needed to be satisfied.

*   *   *

"Would you like a souvenir program?" Wes had to raise his voice to be heard above the echoing voices of the people crowded into the marble-lined foyer of Robinson Auditorium.

Jessie started, turning toward the dark-haired man at her side and shaking her head at the request. Since yesterday afternoon she'd been jumping at shadows. Even a mild-mannered man like Wes could set her off. Or was it because she thought she saw Trevor in the crowd a few minutes ago? All day she'd been imagining him everywhere she looked. As usual, half the population of the city seemed to have turned out tonight, so the man had disappeared into the crowd before she could be sure of his identity.

"Shall we go on in?" Wes solicitously offered her his arm and guided her up the marble stairs and into the theater.

She smiled absently at him, wondering why she didn't find him more interesting. As they walked down the red-carpeted aisle toward the stage, she observed other couples around them. Wes didn't suffer by comparison to the other men, so why did she find him dull? He was nice-looking, attentive, and had a pleasant sense of humor. He wasn't a bore like Connor MacMurray, but she didn't feel any spark of interest when she was with him. She felt almost guilty as he courteously asked her her preference of their two seats, as if she might object to either seat in the center of the tenth row.

The same disinterest was true with Charles Pelinski, candidate number two as Gina called him. He had called her this morning about having dinner over the weekend. She hadn't even bothered to make up an excuse, telling him as politely as possible that she didn't think they really had that much in common. Was Gina right that she was being too particular about her list and needed to consider other candidates? Did Jessie have an unrealistic ideal? She squelched the traitorous little voice inside before another alternative could be considered.

"I hope I brought enough extra hankies, because I just know I'm going to sob through the entire second act," a female voice insisted from close by. "This thing just gets sadder and sadder, and then they all die."

"I can hardly wait, Arnette."

Jessie stiffened in her seat, sure that her imagination was working overtime again. She didn't want to look at the couple approaching her on the right. Hundreds of men in Little Rock had that same mellow voice, maybe even thousands. She held her playbill directly in front of her face, turning toward Wes for good measure.

"You always complain when you take me to the theater, and you know you enjoy it as much as I do," the woman accused, moving closer with each syllable. "I know I caught you sniffling during the finale of *Cats* a few months ago."

"Trevor, how are you?" Wes's question made Jessie want to sink under the seats in front of her. This just couldn't be happening, she thought wildly, and if it was, what had she done to deserve it?

"Good Lord, Wes. Wes Lendall. This is a surprise," Trevor replied from directly in front of her as the two men shook hands. His greeting wasn't enthusiastic. "I haven't seen you since last year's slow-pitch tournament."

"Definitely. Jessica, I'd like you to meet an old opponent of mine. He's one of the sneakiest pitchers in the league."

Only Wes would be delighted over the skill, Jessie decided as she peered over the top of her playbill. The sight of Trevor in his charcoal-gray suit was as unnerving as she expected, making her feel small and vulnerable in her seat. His expression was guarded as he leaned back against the row of seats in front of them. Lowering her playbill slowly, she placed it in her lap and folded her hands over it. "Hello, Trevor."

"Jessie, how are you?" His moderate tone and hooded eyes gave away nothing.

"Oh, do you know each other? It's amazing how everyone seems to know one another in a city the size of Little Rock," Wes declared, oblivious to the tension Jessie thought was crackling in the air. She gripped her hands firmly together in the lap of her terra-cotta silk dress, hoping to steady her jangled nerves.

"Yes, isn't it?" What were the odds of this happening? she questioned rationally on one level while getting up enough nerve to look at Trevor's date on another. She quickly masked her astonishment. She hadn't expected to find a matronly woman, liberal streaks of gray in her neat blond chignon, smiling at her. The woman was old enough to be Trevor's mother. "T.L. hired Aesthetics Ltd. for his new office building, and I've been working on some plans for Trevor's house."

"You must be Jessica DeLord. I'm so pleased to meet you. Both Tory and T.L. have mentioned your work," the lady exclaimed before looking reproachfully at her companion. "No one mentioned you were working for Trevor. If he gives you any trouble, you let me know, dear. I've been handling the Planchet men for over twenty years, now."

"Jessica DeLord and Wes Lendall, this is an old friend of the family, Arnette Montgomery." Trevor made the introduction with a rueful smile as the others nodded in acknowledgment. His shuttered gaze did not change. "Under the guise of housekeeper, she's been terrorizing my family for those twenty years she mentioned.''

"Son, you might want to reconsider that statement." Arnette gave him a measuring look, as if she knew he wasn't up to her weight in an argument. "But only if you ever want to eat another bite from my kitchen or not have your laundry tied in knots."

"I think she has you there, Trevor."

Please let the play start now, Jessie pleaded silently. She wasn't sure how much of this pleasant social chatter she could stand.

"And she has a darn good point, too," Trevor told Wes with a masculine shrug of resignation. "Arnette's also the only person I know that can keep T.L. in line."

"Miz Montgomery, if I can ever be of service, please let me know," Wes stated in awe of her talent.

"Thank you, sir." Her smile for Wes changed into an arch look at the man next to her. "You could learn something from this young man."

"Yes, ma'am." Trevor had a strange expression on his face that Jessie couldn't understand, but she knew that she didn't like it. His attention seemed to be riveted on Wes, as if he took Arnette's last words seriously.

A second later, Jessie breathed a sigh of relief as the lights started to dim, making it unnecessary for Wes to comment, "It looks like they're about to begin."

Glancing over her shoulder, she realized that the theater had completely filled while she had been fixated on her own personal drama. Arnette's next words had her heart plummeting to her knees.

"Trevor, you go ahead and sit there next to Jessica. I'd be tempted to tell her all sorts of incriminating stories about you, and I want to concentrate on the play."

Sucking in her breath, Jessie tried to make herself as small as possible in her plush seat. In spite of her precaution, Trevor's shoulder rubbed against hers as he sat down. The house lights dimmed completely, momentarily leaving the audience in total darkness. By the time the stage lights came on, Jessie had forgotten about her escort, all her awareness centered on the man sitting to her right.

For one irrational moment, she thought of getting up and walking out. Just as quickly she knew that she wasn't capable of making a move or of embarrassing Wes. She was afraid to move in case she brushed against Trevor accidentally. Her skin was already tingling, almost anticipating his touch. Instead of seeing Jean Valjean being persecuted on stage, she was reliving the harrowing moments in Trevor's arms the day before.

She didn't notice that her playbill and clutch purse had slipped to the floor until Trevor moved beside her. When he bent down, then straightened and turned toward her, she didn't understand what he was doing.

"I don't think you want to lose these," he murmured, pressing the two items into her lifeless fingers. For a moment, he seemed hesitant to release her, the warmth of his hands bringing life back to her own.

"Thank you," she whispered, trying unsuccessfully to read his expression in the dim light from the stage. The exchange inexplicably lessened the tension between them, allowing her to ease back in her seat. The figures on stage still made little sense, but she no longer was in a state of panic over what he would do next.

Suddenly other events came into proportion as she reviewed their relationship. He really hadn't done anything outrageous since the night he had returned from Washington. After that, his behavior, while annoying at times, had been fairly normal. She had been letting those early incidents influence her chaotic thoughts. He had done nothing outrageous recently to warrant her apprehension whenever he appeared. Yesterday, although unsettling, had simply been an accident.

The swell of the music and the pandemonium of the students' marching song brought her attention back to the stage. Fleetingly, she was grateful that she had seen the play in New York the year before. She would be able to have a reasonable discussion about the story on the way home. Where had the last two hours gone? she wondered with a momentary panic. Intermission was only a few minutes away.

As the house lights came up, she glanced at Trevor's profile from beneath her lashes. He seemed to sense her action and turned his head, his dark brown eyes only inches from her own. What did she do now?

The decision was taken out of her hands. Wes took control, not seeming to mind that neither Jessie nor Trevor had much to say about the play. Arnette's enthusiasm made up for their silence. There was also a number of acquaintances to be acknowledged, so Jessie didn't have to worry about how to fill the time during the fifteen-minute interval.

As she sat down again, she knew that she would not be going out with Wes Lendall again. Gina had been right, and it wasn't fair to Wes. She was letting the memories of her childhood have too much effect on her adult life. Her candidates weren't the answer to her dilemma. Though she still wanted to have a baby, a family, she knew that she would have to find another solution. Something that wasn't cut and dried; something that made her face her ghosts squarely without jumping at imaginary shadows.

Trevor shifted restlessly next to her. When his shoulder came to rest against hers, Jessie didn't move away from his warmth. For once, she didn't try to fight the sensations caused by his touch. Almost on reflex, she leaned against him, not really aware of what she was doing until his arm stiffened. Hastily she jerked away, crossing her arms in front of her.

What was she to do now? She might have misjudged Trevor, but how did she admit her mistake? It wasn't something that could just be blurted out. How had her life become so mixed up? She had only a simple desire to have a child. Why had it become so complicated? She knew that she had to meet the problem head on, but what about her pride?

When the house lights came up again some time later, she still didn't have an answer.

As Wes exchanged pleasantries with Trevor and Arnette, Jessie tried to think of something significant to say before she left. It was hopeless. Her mind went blank the second she glanced in Trevor's direction. He was looking directly at her, almost willing her to say something. Moving abruptly to break the spell that held her tongue-tied, she dropped her purse again, the contents spilling on the floor.

She quickly knelt down to retrieve her belongings, only to have Trevor move faster. Without bothering to stand up, she watched him collect her possessions and drop them into the black leather purse. When he was done, he seemed to hesitate before returning it to her.

After a brief glance over her head, he seemed to come to a decision. "I've told you I'm not dangerous. Tonight should have proven that. When are you going to admit it?"

She didn't have a chance to say a word before he straightened and escorted Arnette toward the aisle. Wes led her in the other direction, when all she wanted to do was run after Trevor to discover what he meant. Only one thing was clear to her: She was never going to understand Trevor Planchet.

* * *

"That was a nice girl. A little quiet, but a nice girl."

Trevor didn't bother to ask Arnette who she meant as he pulled up in front of her house. He agreed, but all he could think of was Jessie and her stunned expression before he left the theater. Had he finally blown it this time?

"Wasn't it awful when the barricade collapsed and ruined the play? All that blood and gore."

"What?" He turned to his companion to see if she'd lost her mind.

"I just wanted to get your attention," she explained with a gentle smile.

"Why?" He didn't bother to hide his suspicion. The angelic look on her face was all too familiar.

"Because if you let her go out with that Wes person again, I think you're crazy. The young lady would have much rather been with you."

Trevor threw back his head and laughed at her mutinous expression. Although Arnette harped at all the Planchet men about their bad habits, she thought anyone else who didn't adore them needed their heads examined. He climbed out of the car, feeling much better than he had all evening. Knowing Jessie was going out with someone else was one thing; seeing her with the man was another—especially when he knew Wes Lendall was probably a perfect candidate to meet the requirements on her infamous list. Why couldn't her date have been another jerk like the lawyer?

"Don't you worry about Jessie and Wes, Arnette. I plan to do something about that real soon." He helped her out of the car and walked beside her up the front walk. Jessica DeLord was going to have his undivided attention from now on, whether she liked it or not.

* * *

"What's that?" Jessie stopped in the middle of the office Monday morning, suspiciously studying the large box on her desk. Foolishly she began to hope she knew what it was. All weekend she'd waited for a phone call that hadn't been made or a visitor who never came.

"I don't know," her partner responded without looking up from the pile of papers she was frantically sorting through. "It was waiting outside when I got here this morning. Have you seen the Devons' floor plan?"

"No, you had it last." She approached her desk cautiously. The blue-and-white rabbit looked up at her serenely from his corner. Or was it mocking her? Placing her purse and portfolio on the glass surface of her desk, she reluctantly opened the box. Maybe it was simply a lamp or piece of sculpture she and Gina had ordered, she counseled herself as she tore off the plain brown wrapper.

When she pulled back the lid, she discovered her imagined piece of sculpture had fuzzy brown ears. She couldn't contain her smile as she lifted the stuffed animal out of the box.

"Let me guess—a Teenage Mutant Ninja Bunny," Gina commented dryly.

"I think it's a French bunny," Jessie said slowly, wondering how Trevor had found the right accessories. Like a *Les Misérables* character, Monsieur Bunny was wearing a student's distinctive red sash with a pistol tucked rakishly in it; a sword looped on his paw.

"Don't tell me the accountant sent this. There go all my preconceived notions."

"Trevor was at the play, too," Jessie murmured, not bothering to explain further. There was no response. Abandoning her search for a card, she glanced to her right and discovered that she had finally accomplished the impossible. Gina was speechless. "What's the matter?"

The brunette shook her head as if to jump-start her brain. "You actually looked pleased that he sent this one. But more important, why aren't you mad that he showed up at the theater?"

"Why should I be mad? It was a coincidence," she explained while arranging the bunny brothers on the credenza. "I think you're giving him too much credit to think he could manage prime orchestra seats on such short notice. I got the impression he takes Arnette to the theater all the time. Even if he does know Wes, I think it was an accident."

"Arnette? This is getting really interesting," Gina proclaimed, moving around to perch on the credenza. "Is she a blonde, brunette, or redhead?"

"The baby is affecting your brain already," she shot back with a sidelong look of disgust at her friend. "Arnette Montgomery is T.L.'s housekeeper. She practically raised Trevor."

"That's right. His mother died when he was a kid, a heart condition, I think."

"Geez, what have you been doing? Hiring a private detective?" Jessie couldn't believe her ears and gaped at her partner's complacent face.

"I simply asked a few discreet questions here and there." She breathed heavily on her fingernails and rubbed them on her shoulder.

"And?" Jessie prompted a few minutes later when Gina remained mute.

"So you are interested, huh?" Her friend's triumphant smile grated on Jessie's nerves, but she nodded anyway. "Okay, T.L. Planchet has been married three times. The first one produced Sanders and ended in divorce. Can you guess why?"

"Gina, he was only a little boy."

"Probably a very stuffy little boy. Anyway, T.L. married the love of his life next, which gives us Trevor and his sister. Then the second wife died suddenly. Number three was supposed to be a mother to the three kids, but she walked out when her own kid, Curtiss, was in diapers. So this Arnette probably did raise all the kids.''

"You *have* been busy, haven't you?''

"I'm not done yet,'' Gina exclaimed, acting offended at the interruption. "Sanders is married and has his own stuffy little kid named Basil. Yuck. Curtiss is married as well and has two kids. Tory and Trevor are both very conspicuously single, although Tory was engaged about ten years ago. Our man, however, has never ventured into a serious relationship.''

"Don't Curtiss's children have names?''

"Ty Daniel and Amanda Sue,'' she was told readily. "Do I get a prize? Like telling me why you aren't throwing a hissy fit over Monsieur Bunny and the play.''

"I told you it was simply a coincidence, and Trevor was a perfect gentleman.'' She thought Gina was almost as surprised over her behavior as Jessie had been that night. Maybe it would keep her friend occupied so she wouldn't pester her about her new attitude toward the man. At least until Jessie figured out what she was going to do about it.

She wasn't quite ready to eat crow. Gina would find out soon enough that Jessie was anxious to see Trevor in person, not just a long-eared representative. She needed to test her theory.

How was she going to admit anything to him if she couldn't talk to him? That traitorous little voice inside reminded her that she could take the first step. Jessie had gotten as far as placing her hand on the telephone Sunday afternoon, twice, but couldn't go through with it. Whether it was old-fashioned or cowardly, she decided that Trevor was the one who needed to make the next move.

She was going to have to swallow enough of her pride by admitting her mistake in misjudging him. There were times that it was easier to fall back on time-honored customs. Being a Southern lady had its advantages occasionally. She would let Trevor continue to be the man in pursuit, if he would only hurry up and do it.

SEVEN

"The ducks fly at the rise of a harvest moon."

Trevor looked up at the brunette standing next to his table a few hours later. Her jacket collar was pulled up, and she had sunglasses on in spite of the cloudy sky outside and the softly lit interior of the restaurant. She gave a furtive look around the almost deserted room. He frowned as he got to his feet and held out a chair. "Pardon?"

"I thought with your mysterious phone call," Gina explained as she dropped into the chair, "and arranging this cloak-and-dagger meeting that we needed a password. Although I never thought of Bennigan's as a spy's hangout before this."

"I guess I did sound a little like a character from a bad spy movie." He chuckled in answer to her impish smile, beginning to relax for the first time in hours. After he had called Gina to arrange this meeting, he had been assailed by doubts. Did he really want to find out the type of man Jessie was looking for?

"At least you didn't say it was a matter of life or death," she returned good-naturedly. Then her smile disappeared. Narrowing her brown eyes, she gave him a long, hard look. "I hope to heaven your intentions are honorable. That sounds melodramatic, but I mean it. If you hurt Jessie, I'll tear out your heart with a spoon, in the words of my favorite villain."

He knew she meant every single word, but he wasn't offended by her loyal defense of her friend. That was exactly what he would say in her place. In spite of Jessie's regal demeanor, there was also something vulnerable about her that brought all his protective instincts into play. It scared him to death. He'd never felt that strongly about a woman before.

"You have my solemn oath that I'm not playing around," he stated firmly without committing himself too deeply. Gina would undoubtedly misinterpret his confusion over his feelings and walk out. Jessie was too important to him for him to lose out now. "I wish I had someone like you in my corner."

"I think I am." She gave him a chagrined smile. "I wouldn't be here if I wasn't torn between the two of you. I know you'd be good for Jessie, no matter what she thinks she needs."

"Which brings us to the reason for our little meeting." He cleared his throat and straightened his spine against the back of his chair. He had the urge to ask for a cigarette and a blindfold, knowing exactly how a prisoner felt facing the firing squad. This was his moment of truth. "What kind of man does my Jessie want?"

"*Your* Jessie?" He hadn't realized that he'd said the words out loud, but Gina's satisfied grin took away his embarrassment. "Now I don't feel like such a traitor about this." She pulled out a folded sheet of paper from her purse and slipped it across the table.

Sweet heaven, there really is a list. He stared in fascinated horror at the paper, wondering what to do next.

"It isn't going to bite you, you know." Gina tapped the piece of paper with a polished nail. "Jessie's a very organized person, so when she decided it was past time for her to get married, she was as methodical about it as usual. She bought the latest books on relationships and began making a list of what qualities would make a suitable husband."

"The books on the end table," he murmured, still mesmerized by the white rectangle between them. "Why go to all that trouble?"

"She has her reasons, but that's something you're going to have to find out from Jessie." Gina's expression told him that she would go only so far with her help. "If Jessie hadn't been so pleased with Monsieur Bunny this morning, I wouldn't have agreed to come here."

"She liked it?" he couldn't resist asking.

"Yes, she did, but that's all I'm going to say." She didn't have a chance to explain further as the waiter came by to take their orders.

Trevor reluctantly reached for the piece of paper, not bothering to look at it before he folded it and put it in his wallet. He was torn between the desire to read it immediately and the urge to burn it without knowing what Jessie had listed. For now he had to try to have a rational conversation with Gina as they drank the coffee that neither of them wanted.

"This lady has some unrealistic expectations," Trevor announced as he slid into the wooden booth that evening.

Logan looked up from his beer and asked, "So you've met my mother."

"Your mother? What are you talking about?" Trevor glanced up from the sheet of paper in his hand, noticing the morose look on the other man's face for the first time.

"I got back from Texas yesterday to find my mother has been T.L.'s guest for a few days. Damn, I can still hear her asking Uncle Pres, 'Who *are* these people?' when he announced my trip down here." He propped his chin in his hand, and stared balefully at his companion. "She's been alone with Tory for five days now, something I haven't been able to accomplish since I got back. I might as well pack my bags tonight."

"A Yankee retreat? Why couldn't you have had a few ancestors with the same spineless attitude about a hundred and thirty years ago?"

"Those are fighting words, son. I'll have you know I had relatives with Sherman in Atlanta."

"Big deal, so did I. My mother's family is from Maryland," Trevor explained with a smile. "I don't know why I'm trying to cheer you up. All you have to do is corner Tory. I have some big problems. Take a look at this."

Logan sat up and skimmed the typed sheet that was thrust in front of him. He cast a sympathetic look at his friend a few minutes later. "She really does have high standards. Do you fit any of these requirements?"

"My salary and my college degree. And I've never been convicted of a crime," he stated firmly, dismissing three of the twenty prerequisites. At Logan's raised eyebrows, he explained, "A Halloween prank when I was in college that the town folks didn't like. We got off with a stiff warning from the judge."

"Did you find out why she made out this list?"

"Not exactly. Her partner would say only that Jessie is looking for a husband, but I think there's more to it. She was kind of reluctant to give me the list." He sat back to reconstruct the interview with Gina. She had wanted to help him, but would go only so far. The big mystery was why Jessie was looking for a specific type of man. He was on his own to solve that puzzle.

"I don't see anything about babies on here."

"I know, and Gina wouldn't talk about that, either."

"So, what next?"

"I began my challenge last Thursday night. While the next step is doing its work, I'm going to lay low," he informed him, more than pleased with his plan. "I'm going to pique her interest this week but stay safely out of her way. Sort of the water-on-the-stone technique. By the end of the week I think I'll have worn down her resistance."

"Or made her madder than hell," Logan remarked philosophically.

"There is that, but at least she'll know I'm interested."

"This is really serious, then?"

"The vote's still out on that, but I'm more serious about this lady than I ever thought I would be about any woman."

Logan solemnly lifted his bottle of beer. *"Morituri te salutamus."*

"How many of those have you had?" Trevor asked, eyeing his companion closely.

" 'We who are about to die salute you,' " he translated roughly, and shrugged. "It's the only thing I remember from prep-school Latin, and damned if it didn't seem appropriate. Tomorrow I try to get your sister's attention away from her new store."

"Here's to the ladies," Trevor responded solemnly. Was he a certifiable idiot to continue his pursuit? The lady wasn't very encouraging, and her requirements for the perfect male were daunting. Looking at a couple whose arms were entwined by the bar, he knew the answer. The memory of Jessie's hesitant responses to his kisses and the warmth of her willowy body in his arms made it worthwhile. He had to see what other magic she could bring into his life, if nothing more.

"Not another one?" Gina exclaimed as she spotted the third rabbit when she returned from lunch on Wednesday. "He didn't happen to bring it in person, did he?"

"No," Jessie practically snapped. She tried not to look at the hot-pink rabbit sitting next to the others, but her gaze was drawn to it. He was going to pay for this, she pledged silently, shooting a scathing glance at the tiny towel wrapped around the chubby pink waist.

"Should I bother to ask about the towel?"

"No."

"Somehow I thought you would say that," Gina returned morosely. "I have a feeling that you've been holding back some vital pieces of information."

Jessica glared menacingly at her dearest friend.

"How about a message this time?" Gina wasn't going to give up so easily.

"Yes, there was," she answered, her expression still bleak. "He wants me to stop by the house on Saturday—"

"Hey, that's great."

"To discuss his final selections on wallpaper and paint," Jessie finished through clenched teeth as if her friend hadn't spoken.

"You're not real happy about this, are you?"

"I haven't been able to sleep or eat for the past three days. He has me so confused that I don't know what to think anymore."

"I would say he's definitely interested." Gina was always more optimistic.

"In what? Driving me slowly insane? I should have refused to do the house the minute I discovered he was the owner," Jessie grumbled, burying her face in her hands with a groan for added effect. "I could have gone on with my life without Trevor Planchet waltzing in and out whenever he pleases. I also wouldn't be having nightmares about Bugs Bunny chasing me with an ax."

"You *are* in bad shape."

Something in Gina's voice made Jessie splay her fingers and peer suspiciously through them at her friend. "Is there anything you haven't told *me*?"

"Why, heavens no. What would I know about any of this?" Her dark eyes widened in surprise.

"I don't know," Jessie moaned, realizing her mind was turning to mush because of one very elusive male. She was not, however, going to give in. "You've been his biggest cheerleader so far. He could turn out to be an ax murderer as I suggested, and you would still defend him."

"Jessica, how can you say something like that?" Gina laid her hand over her heart to emphasize her innocence, a gesture very reminiscent of the man they were discussing.

"Now you can see the state he's gotten me in. I'm imagining conspiracies all around me," she admitted with a sigh. "I just hope I can last until Saturday. Of course, now that I have six rabbits' feet, I should have good luck."

"I think I'll go make us some tea," Gina announced hastily. "I think this is going to be a long afternoon."

Jessie stepped down from the van on Saturday afternoon, ten minutes before the appointed time. Almost dispassionately, she noticed that her hands weren't quite steady as she reached for her tote bag and the sample books. Uncertain about what lay ahead, Jessie lingered by the car to look at the outside of the house. The painters and roofer had been busy during the week, almost completing the exterior while she had been avoiding the house during the same time.

Trevor had an excellent sense of color, she decided judiciously. Although not showy in the true "Painted Lady" tradition, the house stood proudly among the surrounding oak trees. The body of the house had gone from a dilapidated grubby yellow to a stately grayish taupe, with the structural trim and windows in a creamy dark tan, and the lacework and roof cresting highlighted by a periwinkle-lavender blend. The new colors brought out the alternating textures of the shingles and the carved details of the Eastlake embellishments.

Unable to delay any longer, Jessie climbed the stairs to the porch, her footsteps seeming to echo ominously. Was she about to make an absolute fool of herself? It was too late to back out now. Fleetingly she wished she could muster the aggravation she'd felt a few days ago. Unfortunately, there wasn't time. The front door was open, and he was sure to hear her approach through the flimsy screen.

"Jessie? I'm in the dining room," Trevor called out as if he had read her mind.

Self-consciously she smoothed her hand over her hair, feeling vulnerable with it hanging loose around her shoulders. Were her moss-green slacks and maroon-and-green paisley blouse too casual? Should she have worn a dress instead? She knew she was being ridiculous as she stepped into the entry hall. What did her clothes matter, if she couldn't think of anything to say?

She was brought up short by the furniture that cluttered the dining room. She glanced at the gleaming pieces, realizing this was the collection from the garage she'd inspected last week. Trevor was in the middle of the room, rubbing a cloth over a long rosewood table. From his tousled hair and the way his rust-colored shirt clung damply to his back, he'd been working for quite some time. When he saw her in the doorway, he straightened and leaned his hip against the edge of the table.

"There you are. I thought you got lost for a minute."

"You've been busy this week." Jessie said the first thing that came into her head, then cursed her hasty words. She meant busy working on the house. Would he think she was alluding to the rabbits instead?

"I thought you might want a better look at Aunt Beth's furniture, and then we can discuss what else I need to buy."

She felt silly standing in the doorway but didn't know what else to do. "I hadn't realized there was such a mix of styles."

"Yeah, that's where you'll have to guide me," he admitted. "I know what I like, not what it's called. I figured with the leaves put in the table you could use it as a work area instead of scrambling around on the floor."

"Let's get started, then." Jessie decided that work would keep her mind off the tautness of his shirt across his square shoulders and the way the soft denim of his jeans hugged his lean hips and waist. "From your initial instructions, I've made up two color schemes for each room and did some rough sketches of furniture arrangements. We have about a week to work out a final plan so I can order the wallpaper and curtains."

"Meeting the deadline for the tours isn't going to give you too much trouble, is it?" He moved to her side while she pulled her sketch pad and samples from her tote bag.

"No, I don't think so. I've tried to avoid materials that have to be custom-made." She laid out the floor plan for the lower floor, then the sketches for each room. When Trevor moved closer, she nervously sought a diversion and reached for her pencils in the tote bag.

Her fingers were suddenly clumsy, unable to locate the pencil box quickly. Impatiently she upended the cloth bag, and the acrylic pencil box slipped out easily. "Since you said you preferred mixing contemporary and antique pieces, I've concentrated the brighter, stronger colors and patterns in the rugs and walls. Accent pieces will draw the visitors' eyes to the proper focal points in the room."

"Okay, let's go ahead with these." He quickly gathered up one sketch for each room.

Brushing her hair over her shoulder, she turned toward him to see what else he had to say. He stared back at her, as if he was deferring to her. "Trevor, you can't just make a decision like that. You may hate it a few months from now."

"Why?" His forehead furrowed into a confused frown. "You did all the preliminary work. I told you, I know what I like. I don't like to complicate things, unless absolutely necessary. When I see something I like, I know instantly that's what I want. There's never been anything I've regretted later."

She wasn't sure they were still talking about her work. His eyes had darkened to a polished onyx color, his expression serious as he waited for her protest. "I see. I wish you would take a little more time to decide."

"This is what I want. You have excellent taste and haven't cluttered up the rooms with too much junk." His smile was guileless. He cocked his head to the side and frowned suddenly. "Do you have many customers who change their minds, even if it's too late?"

She couldn't help but laugh. "Of course. They change their minds constantly. That's one of the reasons Gina and I concentrate on corporate clients. There's usually less stress, though an office manager can be just as persnickety or indecisive as a homeowner. Luckily, not too many business people want to match the wall color to a tiny strip in the design of a throw pillow.''

"You mean you do all this work, then change it all around until the client likes it?"

"Of course. That's what I get paid to do. I give the client advice based on my experience," she answered, unable to understand his concern. "Everyone has an image of what they want, and I subtly try to show them how to do it with taste and style. Usually we can send back furniture or drapes, if they aren't custom-made.''

"Have you considered a career in the diplomatic corps?" he asked, giving her a reluctant grin. "I'm beginning to understand why you're so calm and serene. I don't think I've ever met anyone else like you, Jessica DeLord. Don't you ever get hopping mad and want to tell clients where they can put their stupid ideas?''

As he moved closer, she wished she was really the person he was describing. Calm had little to do with her emotions when he was nearby, especially at this moment. Torn between anticipation and apprehension, she willed herself to relax. This was what she had been wanting for the past week, to be face to face with Trevor to test her turbulent feelings.

Raising her chin, she waited for him to continue. Exhilaration shivered through her with one look at his avid expression. She almost laughed out loud at her urge to back away. This was what she'd been fighting against for the past few weeks. How foolish could she be?

It seemed so natural to lean toward him, lean into his hard body as his arms closed around her. The touch of his lips was gentle, hesitant, inviting her to respond. Tentatively she laid her palms against the flat plane of his chest, flexing her fingers against his warmth. His heartbeat matched the acceleration of her own.

Nothing existed in Jessie's universe but the two of them. His arms were taut as his hands brushed over her back. The thin material of her blouse no longer seemed to exist. His unique masculine scent mingled with the smell of lemon oil and swamped her senses. His soft, thick hair slipped easily through her fingers. His mouth parted hers to deepen their kiss, seeking the hidden secrets within.

The traitorous little voice inside her sighed in satisfaction. As Jessie snuggled closer to his strong body, she perceived the danger in him. But instead of retreating, she moved closer, unable to resist the lure.

A moment later she felt bereft when his lips abandoned hers. Then she sighed in delight as his mouth trailed across her cheek to the ultrasensitive skin beneath her ear. "Oh, Jessie, this isn't something that can be put on any list."

For a moment she didn't understand. Why was he talking about her plans for the house at a time like this? Then he was nibbling on her earlobe, and she really didn't care.

"We're good together, aren't we?" His breath, warm and moist at her ear, shivered down her spine. "It doesn't matter if my job involves overnight trips, or if I have two drinks before dinner."

Jessie froze. His words suddenly made horrible sense. He knew about her candidate's list. With sickening clarity, she remembered thinking that Gina had been keeping something from her earlier in the week. Trevor had managed to wheedle the list from her supposed friend!

"Jessie, what's wrong?" Trevor raised his head, still holding her securely in the circle of his arms. His eyes narrowed as he tried to gauge her mood.

"Hey, Trevor! Are you in there, boy?" T.L.'s hearty voice boomed through the quiet room from the back of the house.

When Trevor seemed reluctant to release her, Jessie glared at him. She was not going to lower herself to struggle with him, but she refused to be caught in this embarrassing position. A second later he released her, his movements surprisingly awkward.

"In the dining room," he called, his voice slightly hoarse. He bent down to retrieve the polishing cloth from the floor.

"Hey, boy, this place is certainly shaping up," T.L. announced as he walked into the dining room. Tory and Logan were a few feet behind him.

Jessie thought she saw Logan give Trevor a rather curious look, but she dismissed it. Her imagination was working overtime due to the circumstances. No one would guess that she and Trevor were doing anything besides going over the house plans.

"I'm sorry if we came at a bad time," T.L. declared, almost as if he had been reading Jessie's mind. He brushed by his son's silent figure without a second glance, not bothering to hide his interest in the drawings and samples on the table. "We were out buying an engagement present for Tory and Logan."

"What? When did this happen?" Trevor suddenly came to life, giving his sister and her fiancé an accusing look. Reaching them in a single stride, he hugged his sister and thumped Logan's back enthusiastically.

"Don't you want to know who won the betting pool?" his sister asked, her smiling eyes belying her sardonic tone.

"Ouch! How did she find out?" Trevor stepped back quickly as if his sister might physically assault him. His question was directed at the harassed-looking man next to her.

"I didn't tell her." Logan glared at T.L., who was overly preoccupied with the sketch in his hand. "He wanted to find out if he was the big winner."

"Well, who was?" Trevor demanded impatiently.

"You missed by a day, my friend. Logan proposed on Tuesday night. We didn't tell anyone for a few days while we got used to the idea," Tory replied. She smiled smugly at her brother's disgruntled frown. "So nobody won, and I think it serves y'all right. Jessica, can you believe my family actually bet on when Logan and I would get engaged?"

"I think I can from my experience with your family," she returned quickly, trying not to look in Trevor's direction. Out of the corner of her eye she saw him turning in her direction. "Congratulations on your engagement. I'm sure Trevor wants to show you the house. I can discuss this with him later, so I'll come back—"

"Nonsense, young lady. I'd much rather have some pretty young thing be my guide than my idiot son." T.L.'s broad smile told Jessie that she couldn't refuse. There wasn't going to be an easy escape from this situation.

She felt like a tightly coiled spring that was ready to explode. What made it worse was that no one else, including Trevor, seemed aware of the tension in the room. He continued to tease his sister about being captured by a Yankee, as if he hadn't been kissing Jessie a few minutes ago. Jessie was the only one who felt ill at ease, wanting only to get away to lick her wounds. Unlike Trevor, she couldn't simply switch her emotions off and on.

If T.L. hadn't arrived when he did, she knew she would have done something incredibly stupid. Only a tenuous hold on deeply ingrained good manners was keeping her from lashing out at Trevor now. Why had

she foolishly started to trust him? Whatever brainstorm
had made her soften toward him was now erased.
Hadn't she known she shouldn't let down her guard?
It wasn't her past that made her wary, but the man
himself.

"Hey, where is everyone?" a light soprano voice
called from the front of the house. "We've come to
make an official neighborly call."

A few minutes later the room seemed to be overrun
with people. Everyone seemed to be speaking at once.
Greetings were mixed with congratulations to the newly
engaged couple and questions about what was being
done to the house. Winona Capshaw and her twin sister, Wendy, were gushing over Jessie's ideas and the
delight at seeing her again.

As she led the group through the house, Jessie wondered wildly how she had avoided Trevor Planchet for
so long. They seemed to have a number of friends in
common but had never met until a few weeks ago. First
Abby, then Wes, now Trevor's neighbors Wendy and
Winona, who had been in an interior design class that
Jessie had taught for the University of Arkansas at Little
Rock's adult education program. Though she hadn't
seen them for a few months, the three women occasionally had lunch together. Those irrelevant thoughts kept
her from dwelling on how naturally she and Trevor
worked together while conducting the house tour. To a
disinterested bystander, they might have been a happily
married couple showing off their first home.

"Well, this is splendid, simply splendid," Winona
exclaimed, her arms looped through Jessie's as they
stood on the back deck. "I'm just so glad we dropped
over. Wendy and I were saying the other day that we
hadn't seen you in ages. Isn't that right, Wendy?"

"Exactly," her twin answered in her usual economy

of words. Without another word, she turned to the two men who had accompanied her and her sister.

"I knew the house was getting fixed up, but I didn't know how far sweet old Trevor had gotten. Isn't he just a dear? To think I hated him when we were attending Cotillion."

"Did I hear my name?" Trevor stepped in front of them, blocking the view of the gazebo.

"Yes, you scamp. You always seem to know when women are talking about you." Winona's flirtatious laugh grated on Jessie's already taut nerves. "I was just about to tell Jessie about how horrible you were when we were in school together."

"I was an angel, and you know it. Now what are you trying to blackmail me into doing?"

"I never could get around you," Winona complained with a pout. "I've been looking out my back window studying that little bass boat of yours. It looks so lonely and neglected."

"My boat is yours, Winny," he said gallantly, sketching a courtly bow. "Where are you taking it?"

"Griff and Nolan want to go camping next weekend up at Camp Silver Arrow," she explained succinctly, her coquettish air completely gone. "And darned if Nolan's brother didn't cancel, leaving us without a fishing boat. Say, why don't you come along instead? We were planning on six. What do you think, Wendy? Wouldn't it be great to have Trevor and Jessie come along?"

"Wonderful."

"Oh, Jessie, please say yes. You and Trevor need a reward from all this dusty work." Winona tossed back her blond ponytail with a practiced flip of her hand and smiled ingratiatingly. "I know you two could use the time alone together."

Jessie didn't know what to say or where to look. The group around her was suddenly very quiet, almost expectant. What could she say to her scatterbrained friend that wouldn't sound ugly? She worried the wood flooring with the toe of her shoe. How had she gotten into this mess? By some unknown logic, Winona had decided she and Trevor were a couple. Then Jessie could feel her cheeks begin to burn.

Raising her head, her eyes locked with Trevor's. His almost apologetic expression didn't lessen her discomfort. All too clearly she remembered his explanation last week about neighbors and the lack of curtains. She had a good idea where Winona got her crazy idea.

"I'd say that sounds like a good idea," T.L. pronounced. "Jessie's looking a little puny, and we've probably been working her too hard. A few days of fresh air should do the trick."

Jessie knew that she had to say something, and fast. Winona, with Wendy as her echo, was already making plans. She had to get out of this before it went any further. After today, Trevor Planchet was the last person she wanted to spend any time with, especially on a camping trip. She'd never been camping in her life.

"I would be very careful," Tory Planchet murmured in her ear. Her smile was compassionate at Jessie's start of surprise. "I think T.L. is planning on using the betting pool kitty on Trevor next. Good luck."

Jessie turned and walked into the house for some peace and quiet. She couldn't think of how to turn down Winona's offer, short of refusing at the top of her lungs. Unfortunately, she couldn't bring herself to cause a scene.

"Jessie?" Trevor's voice sounded cautious and unsure, which she knew was ridiculous. He apparently had come into the house directly behind her.

She didn't have time to answer before his family joined them. T.L. wanted to go over every detail of the plans and to find out exactly what was being done next.

Although every minute of the next hour was pure torture for Jessie, she was thankful for T.L.'s forceful presence. He had them discuss each room and what was going to be done. Jessie didn't have to worry about spending additional time alone with Trevor, not with his father standing between them mulling over each and every detail.

She knew that her luck wouldn't continue, judging from the set look on Trevor's face. Concentrating on T.L.'s questions about the ceiling painting she suggested for the living room, Jessie thought wistfully how nice it would have been to plan this house for someone she loved. Anyone but the calculating Trevor Planchet.

She'd almost fallen into his trap but had a lucky escape. So why was she feeling so dejected? Maybe T.L. was right, and she needed some time off. That was why she couldn't resist watching how the afternoon sunlight drew out the reddish-gold highlights in Trevor's thick brown hair. Her fingers flexed automatically at the memory of the silky texture.

Yes, she needed some time off, but not within a thousand miles of Trevor. Unwilling to dwell on her melancholy thoughts, she decided to concentrate her efforts on how firmly but politely to decline Winona's invitation. Even more satisfying was the thought of the tortures that Jessie imagined for her former friend. Gina was going to be sorry she ever heard the name *Trevor Planchet*.

EIGHT

"You have to talk to me sometime, you know," Gina announced from her desk at ten o'clock on Monday morning. She had made the statement every fifteen minutes since she had arrived at nine.

"No, I don't." Jessie didn't bother to turn around. She had come in early that morning and rearranged her office space. Her desk no longer faced the central hub of Aesthetics, Ltd.; she now had a view of a building across the street. Her desk was flush with the wall, and her credenza, conspicuously bare, was within easy reach at her right.

"At least tell me why I'm receiving the silent treatment." Her voice was closer, telling Jessie that her partner had left her desk and was crossing the room.

"The note should be enough." She'd left it in plain sight. The wording had been concise and to the point.

"Okay, I'm deceitful, manipulative, and worse than pond scum. What else is new?"

Jessie tried not to smile at the contrite tone of Gina's voice. She'd planned to remain silent for another half hour, just to teach her meddling friend a lesson. She wasn't really angry, just incredibly annoyed and somewhat embarrassed that Trevor now knew about her list of qualifications.

"Does this have something to do with Trevor, by any chance?"

"As if you didn't know," Jessie accused, spinning around in her chair. Leaning back, she rested her elbows on the padded arms and steepled her fingers together, regarding the culprit through the veil of her eyelashes. "I never knew that you could stoop so low."

"So sue me for wanting to see you hooked up with an incredibly sexy guy. I'm lower than pond scum, which makes me pond silt I suppose." The brunette hung her head in shame, her arms dangling limply at her side. After a moment, she gave Jessie a sidelong look from gleaming brown eyes. "Have I groveled enough?"

"Almost," she stated judiciously. "Now all you have to do is get me out of going camping with the Capshaws, Griff Alexander, Nolan Petrie, and Trevor. I'd forgive you anything for that."

"C—camping? You're going camping?"

"Not if I can help it," Jessie muttered, dropping her hands into her lap. Nervously she fiddled with the gold links of her belt. "I somehow got inveigled into this thing and—"

"And you were too polite as usual to get yourself uninvited," Gina finished accurately. She hiked one hip into the side of Jessie's desk, then crossed her arms over her chest. "Do you really want to get out of this?"

"Of course I do. I don't want to see Trevor Planchet unless absolutely necessary, much less spend a weekend with him out in the wilds." She ruthlessly suppressed all the erotic images that had haunted her during the weekend, when dreams of wilderness camping suspiciously resembled being marooned on a tropical island. Arkansas had waterfalls but not palm trees.

"Should I quote some appropriate Shakespeare at this point?"

"I am not protesting too much. I've never been camping in my entire life."

"It might do you some good," her friend interpolated, a calculating look on her face. "You've been driving yourself too hard, both at work and looking for the ideal daddy. This camping thing may be just the thing—a new environment, fresh air, and relaxation."

"Somehow I really can't take any advice from you seriously these days. I know exactly where your loyalties are," Jessie said dryly. "You'd tell me to book passage on the *Titanic* if Trevor had a ticket."

"So, I made one little slip—"

"That's what the Watergate burglars said."

"Trevor or no Trevor, you need a break," Gina continued ruthlessly. "Any time spent with the Capshaw twins will definitely be entertaining. A little silliness will probably help you get your perspective back and force you to reconsider the desperate measures you've been resorting to, just to find a husband. I'm beginning to think that sperm bank roulette might not be a bad idea after all. Oh, and I'll help you move your desk back after lunch."

Giving a decisive nod to indicate she was through, Gina hopped off Jessie's desk and walked back to her desk. Jessie watched her morosely for a few minutes, not wanting to admit that some of what she said made sense. She did need a break. During all the years she'd been pushing herself, she'd only taken a day or two off occasionally, never a real vacation. She didn't think, however, a camping trip was the answer.

For a second she was tempted to pull the mirror out of her desk drawer. She wanted to see if she looked like she was at death's door, since both T.L. and Gina had mentioned she looked worn down. Of course, if she could just get a decent night's sleep without dreaming of Trevor, crazy rabbits, or romantic waterfalls, maybe she would look perfectly healthy.

Hadn't she lain awake the past two nights cursing her stupidity in even considering giving Trevor a chance? The traitorous little voice told her that he'd gone to Gina only because he truly cared for Jessie. She didn't think so. He was just trying to assure himself of another conquest. Then why didn't he try to be a sterling example of her ideal, the little voice countered. She knew that it was too much effort for someone who relied on easy charm.

So why was she so disappointed that she was right?

"Delivery for Jessica DeLord."

For a moment Jessie thought the muffled voice came from the four-foot rabbit in front of her desk, then she noticed human legs below the big white feet. Before she could speak the rabbit lurched forward to land on top of the papers on her desk. Her new pet was yellow and white with a bright yellow backpack strapped to its pudgy body.

"He's ready for the trip, Jessie. Are you?" Trevor asked smoothly, casually leaning one arm on her desk alongside the rabbit.

He was the last person she expected to see. When she'd been at the house the past few days, he'd left curt messages concerning the schedule of what needed to be done before the Candlelight Tour. The landscaper would be finished by Friday. On Tuesday, the painter would leave an estimate for painting and papering the interior. Wednesday, Trevor would be at a meeting with the house chairman, who would be overseeing the necessary details for the house on the night of the tour. Now on Thursday he was standing in her office. Why hadn't she given in to the impulse of leaving him a note of her own—her letter of resignation.

"Do you own a toy store?" she asked for lack of anything else to say.

"It's beginning to look that way. I'm on a first-name basis with the entire staff by now," he answered easily, not bothering to misunderstand. "You didn't answer my question? Are you ready to go camping?"

"You didn't have any luck getting hold of Winona, either?" She addressed the question to the rabbit, knowing it was safer that way.

"Nope. Remember she wants my boat." She saw him move out of the corner of her eye, leaning his hip against the side of her desk as he waited for her response.

"She doesn't want anything from me, but she still won't return my calls." Jessie didn't bother to hide her frustration over the matter. "I've left ten messages on that darn machine."

"The easiest thing might be to go," he said softly. "What can it hurt?"

For the first time she looked directly at him. As usual when he had her cornered, she couldn't read his expression. Sometimes she felt like the only time he let her know what he was thinking was when he kissed her. Ruthlessly suppressing the sensations that that thought conjured up, she wondered what her next move should be. If only he didn't look so darn good, she protested mutely, trying not to notice the material of his tan slacks over his muscular thigh, or the tantalizing V at the open neck of his shirt. The man should be outlawed.

At least he hadn't told her she looked like death warmed over.

"I'm not dangerous, Jessie, just a little impulsive now and then," he murmured, his hooded eyes giving nothing away as he leaned toward her. "I'd never hurt you intentionally. I think you know that. Prove it to me by going on the camping trip."

Mutely she stared at his impassive face, almost drowning in his chocolate-brown eyes. It was fear that was making her hands tremble. Clasping her fingers tightly together, she met his gaze with a level look. He was willing her to refuse, willing her to tell him whether she was afraid of him or herself. She wasn't going to do it.

The camping trip might not be such a bad idea, she rationalized. It was simply a weekend with a group of people, and there was safety in numbers. She could spend the weekend proving to him that she was immune to his charm once and for all. The idea was a challenge to her resolve. Was she brave enough to meet it?

"All right, Trevor. I'll be glad to go," she stated clearly, wanting to be sure that he understood her. Raising her chin slightly, she smiled at the surprise he couldn't quite hide. Inwardly she let out a sigh of relief that she had made the right decision.

"No conditions?" He quirked an eyebrow, almost daring her to give him a list.

"No conditions, no prerequisites," she answered firmly. She was done with lists, whether they were to find a potential father or to provide conditions for working with him. Trevor and she would meet as equals, with nothing between them.

A ghost of a smile curved his lips, drawing her gaze inexorably to it. "That sounds good to me, sweetheart. I'll pick you up at five o'clock tomorrow night."

Fleetingly, as he sauntered toward the door, Jessie wondered if she was being a fool again. Silently she chanted, *It's only a camping trip, not a survival test.* Had bad could it be? There would be other people around. The scenery and camping facilities in Arkansas were acclaimed for their beauty and comfort. A little weekend trip in a camper wouldn't be so bad, or maybe they would stay at one of the lodges. She would be able to keep plenty of space between her and Trevor.

The traitorous little voice asked her if she really wanted to keep her distance. Of course, she did. That was why she'd agreed to go on this trip, wasn't it?

"We're here," Trevor announced, turning the car into a culvert at the side of the dusty road.

"We're where?" Jessie looked out the window of the land rover and didn't see much of anything in the twilight but trees, lots of trees, and the glimmer of water beyond.

"This is where we're going to camp." He didn't elaborate, but simply pressed the heel of his hand against the horn. Then he was climbing out of the car and waiting. A shout from beyond the rise answered the honk, and a minute later Griff Alexander, a lantern in his hand, came into view.

"Glad to see you could find it," he called.

"No problem. Your directions were great," Trevor called back, giving Jessie, still sitting in the passenger seat, a curious look. He shrugged and went to work on releasing the struts that secured the bass boat to the top of the rover. "This is really back and beyond."

"That's why we like it. It's away from all the sissy campers who want a TV and a microwave while they're out roughing it," Griff told him, a derisive smile on his face.

What's wrong with wanting a few creature comforts? Jessie wanted to ask as she reluctantly scrambled out of the vehicle. Why hadn't she asked more questions? Because Arkansas was nationally renowned for its state park system and camping facilities. The state was filled with lodges and cabins that had long waiting lists for occupancy. Besides, it was incredible to think the Capshaw twins were in to roughing it. "Where are Winona and Wendy?"

"They're helping Nolan get the shelter cleaned out."

"Sh—shelter?" She wasn't sure she wanted to know the answer, though she was relieved he hadn't said *tent*. Until now she'd been hoping that Griff had a warped sense of humor and that there was a solidly built cabin with all the modern conveniences she had imagined all week.

"We don't get that carried away with the back-to-nature stuff," Griff explained, dashing the last of Jessie's hopes, while helping Trevor unload their supplies. Winona had finally called on Thursday night to give Jessie a list of foodstuff to bring and what type of clothing to wear. "This was a scout camp years ago and part of it has been condemned, so pay attention to the signs if you're out wandering around. The rest is rented to campers. We use the shelters that were built for the kids. That allows for a few amenities like flush toilets and running water, even if it is cold."

"How nice," Jessie murmured as her heart plummeted to the soles of her new high-tops. It didn't help that she thought she saw Trevor's lips twitch as she took two grocery sacks from him. Could she steal the keys from him and head straight back to the city? Then she realized that she had no idea where they were. After Trevor had turned off Highway 70, there had been too many twists and turns to count in the gathering darkness.

It couldn't get any worse, she decided as she trudged up the barely visible trail behind the men. Deep in a conversation about bait and lures, the two men didn't see the irony of the formation as Jessie did. Was there some truth in the new theory about men secretly wanting to go back to their primitive forebears? She certainly felt like she had stepped back in time as she walked a good four paces behind. Or had she been reading too many pseudo-psychology books lately?

"There you are. We were beginning to wonder if you got lost," Winona called from the opening of the shelter. It was a concrete structure with three sides. The building was one large room partitioned into four areas. A stone fireplace, giving off a welcoming glow, stood to the right under the wooden overhang of the structure.

"Hello," Wendy sang out from next to Nolan. They were standing toward the back of the shelter near a wooden frame that Jessie couldn't quite make out. Like her sister, Wendy was dressed in a faded cotton shirt and jeans as well as sturdy ankle boots, a far cry from the sophisticated fashions they normally wore. Was it any wonder Jessie hadn't anticipated playing Wilderness Family over the weekend?

She was very conscious of her newly purchased jeans, even though she'd washed them several times to get the stiffness out. Everyone else looked like they'd owned their outdoor gear for years. Trevor's jeans were soft, almost white from countless washings, and hugged his hips and legs like a second skin. His chamois shirt had once been deep green but now was faded as well. The scuffs on his leather boots told the same story.

"Okay, now that we're all here, we can get our jobs assigned." Winona stood in the middle of the shelter like a general calling the troops to order on the eve of a battle. "Jessie, do you mind cooking breakfast? Wendy and I will take care of lunch and dinner. I know it sounds so damn reactionary, but I'd rather cook than chop wood and gut fish, wouldn't you?"

"Definitely," she answered, dropping the shopping bags on the countertop along the wall near the fireplace. As her eyes adjusted to the dark interior, she began to notice some disquieting details while Winona continued to reel off instructions. The wooden frames that occupied most of the space in each partitioned area were bed frames—double bed frames. Wendy and Nolan had just finished pumping air into two air mattresses and had placed them side by side on a frame. The couple was unrolling a double sleeping bag over the mattresses.

Calculating quickly, she counted only three sleeping areas. The fourth section at the front of the shelter was a makeshift kitchen with cupboards and a countertop. Griff had mentioned a bathroom, which was probably in the back near the interior fireplace, she decided. She didn't need any prodding from her traitorous little voice for her next revelation. The sight of her overnight bag sitting snugly next to Trevor's canvas bag at the foot of the nearest bed frame was all she needed to know. It didn't take a rocket scientist to figure out she was supposed to share sleeping quarters with him.

At precisely that moment Trevor looked up from untying one of the sleeping bags. Even in the dim light she could tell he knew exactly what she was thinking. He was probably waiting to see her reaction. Two could play this game, she decided with an unnatural calm, but almost changed her mind at Griff's next words.

"Hey, Trev, you might as well zip those sleeping bags together now. You'll need the extra warmth of shared body heat in the middle of the night when the fires burn low. It gets damn chilly."

Jessie looked down at her shoes and wondered for an irrational moment if she could run screaming into the night without losing her self-respect. Taking a deep breath and biting on her lower lip, she went to help Winona unpack the food supplies, knowing that Griff's words made perfect sense. She might not like what he said, but she was a rational, mature adult who had been brought up to rise above adversity in a calm and controlled manner. A lady never raised her voice or created a scene, no matter what the provocation.

With a sidelong glance at Trevor's head bent over the two sleeping bags, she wondered if her mother had considered a situation like this when she had counseled her children on proper, polite behavior. Concentrating on stacking canned goods on the shelf, Jessie determined that she would survive this weekend, no matter what, and with dignity. The bed frame was nice and wide with plenty of room for two people to sleep comfortably without getting in each other's way.

Three hours later she was having second thoughts. Just once in her life maybe she could forget her dignity and throw a screaming, raucous fit. Or else, she silently told her reflection in the cracked mirror, she could calmly go out and get in bed with Trevor Planchet.

"Hey, Jessie, did you go to sleep in there?" Winona yelled through the wooden door to the bathroom.

"I'm on my way out," she returned, knowing that it was now or never. Tightening the sash on her terry-cloth robe, she took a deep breath and opened the door.

"I'm so glad y'all came along," the other woman exclaimed as she slipped through the door. "We really should do this more often." Thankfully she closed the door before Jessie could give her an honest answer.

"Not on your life," she mouthed, just in case anyone else was close at hand. Walking slowly toward the partition, as if she was about to face the Spanish Inquisition, Jessie was relieved to see the three men were still sitting on camp stools near the fireplace outside. The sight of the fire made her aware of how chilly the shelter had become since the sun had set. It made perfect sense to have a sleeping partner to ward off the cold night air.

As she walked to the side of the double bed frame,

Jessie wondered for the hundredth time how she'd managed to get herself into this predicament. Was Gina sitting at home sticking pins in some kind of magic doll? Right now it seemed entirely possible as she looked at the two sleeping bags that were zipped together and lying over the air mattresses. There wasn't anything she could do but go to bed.

Hastily she shucked her robe and climbed under the down covering. Even in her flannel nightshirt she shivered. Whoever decided that camping was fun? She wiggled and tugged until she was sure she was covered from her neck to her toes.

"It will be warmer in a few minutes," Trevor said from above her, long minutes later, "once the sleeping bag distributes your body heat."

She rolled over onto her side to block out the disturbing sight of Trevor stripping off his nylon jacket to reveal his form-hugging sweatsuit. But it was worse listening to the rustling sounds and letting her imagination go into overdrive. A cool blast of air hit her back, telling her what she already knew—Trevor was lying down beside her. She willed herself to relax, not to give a hint that her blood pressure had gone sky high or that her nerves were stretched to their limit.

"Jessie, I'm sorry about this. I really didn't know."

His mellow whisper didn't help her equilibrium. He was turned toward her, his breath tickling the back of her neck. She didn't want to admit that this wasn't his fault, but sometimes she was too honest for her own good. "I know."

"At least I can prove to you for once and for all that I can be a gentleman."

A giggle from either Wendy or Winona saved her from answering. It didn't matter to her what the night would prove, because she knew that she would probably be a certified lunatic by morning. Just as he had promised, she was feeling warmer. In fact her entire back felt like it was on fire, ignited by the heat of Trevor's body. She could clearly remember the imprint of his long, lean frame along her back that day outside his bedroom.

An owl sounded in the distance, and she could hear the sounds of other nocturnal animals scurrying past the shelter. She didn't dare close her eyes. If she did, she would begin to imagine what was outside the shelter, or what could happen inside the sleeping bag if she rolled over just a few inches. Another giggle sounded in the darkness, and Jessie bit back a groan. Would she be branded a coward for life if she went and slept in Trevor's land rover with the doors locked?

Trevor rolled onto his back and, as the wooden frame creaked, wondered if he was getting too old for this sort of thing. Or was that his body that creaked? Stretching to get the kinks out, he suddenly froze in place. He was alone. Jessie's soft, warm body wasn't beside him. Then a sound from the front of the shelter caught his attention.

He propped himself up on his elbow. Jessie was standing in front of the fireplace preparing breakfast. Fleetingly he wondered if she had slept any better than he had. Every hour he had found himself staring at the ceiling. Usually a sound sleeper, he seemed to need reassurance that Jessie was still beside him. Or was it a punishment for asking her to come on this trip?

He always considered Winona Capshaw a ditz, but he couldn't blame this insanity on his silly neighbor. What had he expected by going camping with two engaged couples—a boys' and girls' dormitory? Though he'd apologized to Jessie for his mistake, was he really all that sorry?

Certainly not about an hour ago when he had waked.

At first he had thought he was dreaming, but the feel of Jessie in his arms had been too real, too intoxicating. During the hour before dawn, she had turned to him, her head fitting perfectly into the curve of his shoulder. Her palm had been spread over his heart, and for a moment, he had wondered if the rapid beat of his pulse would wake her. She had stayed curled up in his arms like a trusting child while he had gritted his teeth and tried to go back to sleep.

Knowing it was insane to remain in the sleeping bag with the lingering scent of Jessie pulling at his senses, Trevor roughly tossed back the covers. Grabbing up his extra set of clothing, he padded to the bathroom. If he was smart, he'd go take a polar dip in the lake to calm down his body.

"You look like you're used to cooking for an army," he remarked ten minutes later as Jessie deftly measured oatmeal in her hand. She dumped the raw oats into the boiling caldron of water and dusted off her hands.

"I'm the oldest in a large family, so I guess you can say I am used to cooking for an army, though I'm a little out of practice," she answered easily, revealing to him that she didn't remember those precious minutes before dawn. She looked about ten years old with her hair in a ponytail and very little makeup. "I also used to sub in the kitchen when I was waitressing my way through college."

"I remember now, the picture on the table. How many kids were there?" He joined her at the worktable as she began slicing melons. Faintly he could hear the others stirring behind them, and it disappointed him. This was probably the only time he would have alone with Jessie for the rest of the day.

"The final count was ten," she answered shortly, seeming much more interested in the melon.

He was intrigued. For some reason he'd pictured her

as an only child, a pampered little girl carefully taught the very precise manners that made her seem so regal. He wanted to know more. "Wasn't your father a farmer?"

She looked up then, her blue eyes dark and troubled. For a moment she hesitated, then apparently came to a decision. "He was a bigamist."

The word hung between them. He didn't know what to say. What did anyone say in response to such a statement? Words of sympathy would sound hollow, since he had no way of knowing the turmoil she had gone through.

"How old were you when you found out?" he found himself asking, and knew he surprised her by the way her eyes widened before she bent over the melons again.

"I was twelve. My mother had an emergency appendectomy." Her voice was so low that he had to bend his head to catch the words. "Daddy was a traveling salesman with a company that was headquartered in Chattanooga. I called the main office and a man there gave me a phone number to call in Knoxville. The woman who answered the phone said she was Mrs. DeLord, and she would be glad to take a message for her husband."

"Damn."

"That's sort of how I felt at the time," Jessie murmured. "It really can't be much worse than when your mother died. How old were you, Trevor?"

"I was eight." He remembered his sense of betrayal and loss when the woman he thought of as a smiling angel was taken away from him. At least he had good memories to sustain him over the years. All Jessie had was the betrayal. Now he understood her list for a prospective husband. She was trying to avoid a second disaster in her life.

"What happened?" He couldn't let it drop. He knew that talking about it was important to both of them.

"When mother recovered she contacted the other wife in Knoxville. We were living outside Jackson in a house that belonged to my grandparents." Jessie moved back to the fireplace, working automatically as she told the story. "Mama and Aunt Lena, as we came to call her, pooled their small reserves of money and hired a lawyer. After Daddy went to jail, we all moved in together. My family with four kids and the other with six. It's probably the best thing my father had ever done for us. He died six months after he was paroled." Jessie stirred the oatmeal methodically then took a deep breath and continued. "It was nice to have two adults around, and more sisters. I'd been outnumbered three to one before, and it evened out the odds."

"Hey, is breakfast about ready? All this fresh air makes me ravenous."

At that moment Trevor wanted to dump the entire pot of oatmeal on Winona's tousled curls. Then he saw Jessie's slight smile and relaxed. This new harmony between them hadn't been shattered. He had to learn to curb his impatience. Which, he acknowledged ruefully, is what had caused all his trouble in the first place. They had the rest of the weekend, and beyond. Didn't they?

"Come on, Wendy, sing us another one," Jessie called across the campfire they'd built down by the lake. The fishermen had been triumphant, claiming that the trout had been so happy to see them that they had almost jumped into the boat. Dinner had been a feast of fried fish with all the fixings.

After some good-natured bickering, the men had grudgingly cleaned up. Winona had rewarded their efforts by producing marshmallows, graham crackers, and chocolate bars for dessert. She also conned the men into toasting the marshmallows, claiming that it was man's work.

Jessie settled back against her rock, licking the last remnants of gooey marshmallow and melted chocolate from her fingers. "Did you really learn that song at scout camp?"

"Are you kidding?" Wendy had become more talkative as the day had progressed. "That little ditty was from my summers in Branson at Silver Dollar City. I danced and sang my way through college."

"Lucky you. I worked as a waitress forever to get my sister and me through college," Jessie returned, trying to pretend she didn't see Trevor dropping down beside her. His hip brushed against hers as he settled into place, but she kept her eyes trained on the fire in front of them.

"Both of you?" Winona and Wendy asked together.

"We went in pairs, each one working to help the other. Betsy and I were the oldest," Jessie explained, not bothering to mention they hadn't started college until their mid-twenties.

"Well, I don't know about you folks, but all this exercise and fresh air has made me really sleepy," Griff announced before pouncing on Winona, who squealed in delight at his attack.

"That's subtle, Alexander," Nolan called from the other side of the fire, where Wendy was snuggled close to his side. "I think I need to take a walk before turning in. Don't you think so, sweetheart?"

"Definitely," she said, unable to contain her giggle.

Jessie wasn't sure what to do. If Winona and Griff wanted some time alone, she couldn't go back to the shelter. She shivered against the cool night breeze. Next to her, Trevor was incredibly still and quiet. Helplessly she watched the two couples scramble to their feet.

"We'll take care of the fire," Trevor announced suddenly, almost making Jessie squeak in surprise. "Y'all take the supplies up, and we'll be all set."

"The man has no romance in his soul, making me carry garbage," Griff grumbled good-naturedly as they gathered up the picnic basket, cooking supplies, and trash bags.

"I do, too," Trevor countered. "I'm getting someone else to carry the garbage, aren't I?"

As the others disappeared into the trees, Jessie tried not to react nervously. She was a rational adult who didn't think Trevor was going to pounce on her the minute the others were out of sight. Of course he wasn't. They would simply sit here and have a nice, quiet talk.

"Boo!"

Jessie shrieked and would have jumped to her feet if Trevor hadn't caught her by the shoulders. Her breathing labored and her heart leaping into her throat, she turned on him and pummeled his chest with her fists. "Are you crazy?"

"No, I just wanted to get all this skittishness out of the way," he explained matter-of-factly, his hands anchored firmly on her shoulders. "You've fidgeted from the moment you realized we were going to be alone together. Now we can relax and just sit here and quietly talk."

Jessie shook her head in wonder. She didn't think she was going to understand this man in a million years, but she realized that he'd done exactly the right thing. All her reservations seemed to have melted away abruptly. The tension miraculously lifted, and Trevor immediately sensed it. His hands gently squeezed her shoulder.

It seemed natural a few minutes later when he turned her and settled her back against his chest, his arms linked around her waist. "Tell me about growing up with ten kids in the family. I thought four was a madhouse. Ten must have been murder."

She responded to his gentle demand, talking easily about her family for the first time in years. Telling him about her father that morning had released something inside, letting her face her ghosts, as Gina would say. She talked about the good times and the bad.

It was a perfect night, she decided with a contented sigh, listening in turn to Trevor talk about his childhood. The sky was clear with hundreds of stars twinkling overhead, sparkling in the lake along with the half moon. The cool breeze wasn't a bother as long as she was sitting next to the fire with Trevor's arms keeping her warm. Tonight was a time that she wanted to capture in a bottle. She could snare the beauty of the moment and take it out later to luxuriate in the magic again and again. It was a special night; she didn't have to think about yesterday or tomorrow, only the moment.

NINE

Jessie didn't want the moment to end. She felt lethargic, floating on a cloud of sensations, hot and forbidden. Threading her fingers through the silky substance of Trevor's hair, she encouraged him to deepen their kiss. He was the source of her languor, making her blood flow like warm molasses to the heated core of her yearning.

His skin felt like roughened velvet as she trailed her fingers over his chest and arms. She couldn't get close enough to assuage the burning need that he kindled with his clever fingers and drugging kisses. Parting her lips, she allowed him to plunder the secret depth, beginning an exploration of her own that could take forever. She was a smoldering ember that he was bringing to life, fanning her internal heat. Any minute she would burst into flame.

Twining her arms around his waist she moved closer, but not close enough. With restless movements, she tried to show him what she wanted, what they needed. To appease the aching hunger simmering low in her abdomen, she rubbed against the hard length pressing between her legs. She couldn't contain her purr of satisfaction.

"Hey, rise and shine, everybody! The sun's a'wastin'."

Jessie's eyes snapped open, meeting the passion-glazed brown eyes directly below hers. For a moment she was disoriented, then reality came crashing into focus. She was lying on top of Trevor, not merely resting, but with her body clinging and molding to his contours.

Nolan was the one who had given the morning call, she realized, but didn't dare look around to see who else was up.

Suddenly everything went dark. She reached out automatically for something stationary, an anchor in the unknown. Her wandering fingers encountered warm, taut flesh. "Jessie, please be still for a moment."

Trevor's hoarse plea froze her in place once more. Her mind and body were now fully awake. He had pulled the sleeping bag over their entwined bodies, out of sight of the others. Unfortunately it only alleviated one of their problems. She was still draped across his chest with her legs tangled intimately with his. The slick perspiration between their bodies told her that they had been clasped together for some time. With the two of them trapped under the down covering, the heat was intensifying. The darkness magnified her sense of touch, making her all too aware of every inch of their bodies pressed together in the confined space.

"Come on out, y'all. We got more fish to catch today." It was apparent that Nolan was having trouble suppressing the amusement in his voice, making Jessie want to wear the sleeping bag over her head for the rest of the trip. "You, too, Griff and Winona. Let's get crackin'."

"Jessie, just slide very carefully over to your left," Trevor whispered, his hands resting lightly at her waist.

His hands touched bare skin, making Jessie all too aware that her nightshirt had ridden up.

"Okay, here I go," she managed to croak. Desperately, she tried to remember what had been reality and what had been fantasy. Her troubled thoughts were the least of her worries as she awkwardly attempted to maneuver across the disturbing body beneath hers. A moment later she was on her side of the bed, wondering if the groan of relief had been hers or Trevor's.

She huddled under the shield of the sleeping bag while Trevor got up. Her senses went back into overdrive at the sight of his sweat pants riding low on his hips before he hiked them back in place and tightened the drawstring. Had she untied it during the night? She could feel her cheeks flame at the thought.

"I'll be done in the bathroom in a few minutes," Trevor said softly, then surprised her by leaning over to brush his lips across her damp forehead. He sauntered away with his change of clothes held squarely in front of him.

This was exactly what she had been afraid of by being thrown into the company of Trevor Planchet, Jessie groaned inwardly, brushing her tousled hair out of her face with an unsteady hand. *Mmmm, it certainly is,* responded the traitorous little voice. She squelched every memory and thought that wasn't to do with getting out of bed with as much dignity as possible.

Now all she had to do was get through the rest of the day, if she could. Everyone else seemed to be preoccupied with gearing up for the morning, she noted with relief as she shrugged into her robe. Griff gave Winona a smacking kiss under Nolan's interested gaze, unconcerned about his ribald comments. Could she be as nonchalant?

As she passed Trevor on the way to the bathroom, she experimented with a carefree smile. It was a dismal failure, judging from his somber response. For someone who prided herself on having impeccable manners, she certainly had no idea how to handle a situation like this. She doubted that Miss Manners had an example on how to apologize for mauling a man in his sleep.

He didn't know what to say now that they were alone together. The others seemed to have conspired against them all day, separating them for hours or never leaving them alone. Trevor surreptitiously watched Jessie as he steered the car along the mountain road. Somehow he didn't think saying, "This morning was great. Want to do it again sometime?" had the right ring to it. Jessie didn't always appreciate his humor.

If he had given in to his first impulse this morning, he would have bundled her, sleeping bag and all, into the rover and headed for the nearest motel. A real romantic he was, he thought morosely.

Now, ten hours later, he was still reeling from the impact of waking up to Jessie's ardent kiss. He always suspected there was a deep well of passion inside her, but this morning told him that he hadn't had a clue. A twenty-four-hour dip in the icy waters of the lake probably wouldn't have helped him recover. Looking at her averted profile, he knew that he couldn't bring up that subject. So, when in doubt, go for the mundane.

"Are we going to be able to get everything ready for the tours in two weeks?" Did the question sound as lame to her as it did to him?

"Hmm, oh, I think so." Her voice was barely a thread of sound before she cleared her throat. Trevor wondered in a moment of panic if she was on the verge of tears. Why had he pressured her into coming this weekend? "The painter starts tomorrow, and should be done by the end of the week. You're certainly paying him enough."

"I've been told by Mrs. Langford-Hughes that Timothy is an *artiste*, a regular virtuoso with his brush—whatever that means. Apparently his brother has an equal talent with wallpaper, so I guess I'm paying for quality as well as quantity."

"I hope so."

Now what do I do? Do I promise her that I'll never hurt her the way her father did? Trevor had always been monogamous in his relationships, but he didn't think testimonials from the women in his past would be such a hot idea.

"Well, the landscaping is done." That was brilliant, Planchet. Trees and shrubs are always a real conversation rouser.

"It looks wonderful."

"When will the furniture get here?" Yet another conversational winner, he decided, but he would rather talk about the house than return to the oppressive silence.

"I think the first delivery should be Friday. The Dallas warehouse had all the bedroom pieces in stock," she answered matter-of-factly, sounding almost normal to Trevor's sensitive ears.

Could he lead into something more personal now that they were discussing bedroom furniture? A quick look at his companion's patrician profile said no. But at least she wasn't turned away from him anymore.

"What about the rest of the stuff?" Stuff? Was that the best he could do? He couldn't care less about the furniture; his sole interest was the decorator.

"That should be here by the middle of the following week. If everything goes all right, I'll have three full days to make sure all the pieces are in place. The drapes will be delivered the day before the tour."

"That's cutting it awfully close."

"A little, but what's a little stress among friends?

The drapes are the least important accessory. It won't matter too much if they aren't up."

Did he imagine that her tone was forced? "Jessie, I'm sorry I've dumped all this extra work on you. I had no idea what was involved. I'm used to going to the store, picking out something, and taking it home."

"Well, you are still going to do some of that," she stated, a slight trace of humor in her voice. "I've compiled a list of linens as well as a few items for the kitchen and the bathrooms that you get to shop for. I'm not one of those decorators who pick out personal items for clients. I just gift wrap your possessions."

The only item he wanted gift wrapped right now was sitting next to him.

"Don't worry about too much work. It's been kind of fun working on a domestic project, especially on a deadline like this." Jessie scooted down in the seat, seeming much more approachable than she had all day. Was she forgetting about this morning? "It was a real challenge to my professional pride."

Trevor considered the word *pride*. Was there too much pride involved in their relationship, professional and personal? As he changed lanes for the entrance ramp to the interstate, he speculated on what he would have to do to breach Jessica DeLord's pride while soothing her vulnerability. Did he have the ability to handle such a complex matter?

For now, he was leaning toward emotional cowardice. "The house chair will be getting in touch with you the week of the tour. She has the florist lined up and wants to set up a meeting with the tour guides, probably Thursday night before the tour. They can go over the house and estimate how long each group will take to go through the house. Mrs. Langford-Hughes thinks there will be a large turn out this year with a number of older houses on display for the Candlelight and the day tour.''

"That's nice." Jessie's answer was slurred. When Trevor turned to ask if she wanted to stop for dinner at the next exit, he discovered that she had fallen asleep. So much for his anxiety about what to say, he decided with a humorless smile. She was so concerned about what had happened this weekend, she couldn't stay awake.

Trevor frowned as he looked down at the card in his hand early the next morning. He studied what he had written, wondering if it was enough and knowing it wasn't what he wanted to say. A man just didn't write something like that on a card to enclose with a gift. Would Jessie read between the lines? Would she want to? Looking down at the green rabbit snugly tucked in a plaid sleeping bag, he was torn. What else could he write but "Thank you for a wonderful weekend. Will call when I get back in town''?

"Another one, Trevor? I would have thought the other four bunnies would have been more than enough," the woman behind the counter stated. With one look at his confused frown, she continued, "They're hearty little breeders, so only two would be necessary."

The clerk shrugged when he didn't laugh and silently rang up the sale. She didn't bother to ask where it was to be delivered. Trevor thanked her absently and walked out to his car. After climbing into the driver's seat, he waited before starting the engine. He knew that he was cutting the time short. His flight to Tampa left in about forty minutes, but traffic would be light by now.

Trevor had forgotten about the trip until his boss had called late last night to go over some last-minute details. It didn't matter to him. He had more important things to worry about than covering the end of spring training. The professional baseball season would start with or without him, and it certainly wasn't as important as falling in love with Jessie DeLord. That was the most important thing in the world to him, and now he had to leave town.

He wasn't sure when it happened, possibly the moment he'd looked across the room at the Bushes' party and saw a princess in red satin. Or had it been the night she was sitting on his dining room floor looking like she belonged there? He knew for certain the night by the campfire. The certainty had grown steadily all the next day. When she told him about her family, he'd wanted to hold her and wipe away all the hurt she had known. Her usual self-assurance had disappeared, leaving only the vulnerability.

At that moment, the growing bud of love deep inside him had started to unfurl. He knew why he'd been so persistent, so dogged in his pursuit. Without acknowledging the true reason, he simply knew he couldn't let her out of his life. His happiness, his well-being, his very existence now depended on having Jessica DeLord by his side.

And all he had to do was prove to her that he wasn't just another charming, irresponsible man that could make her life miserable. He'd certainly shown her what a perfect fool he could be. Was it too late?

The memory of waking up yesterday morning with Jessie's tantalizing lips on his, her body soft and sultry in his arms, was his single ray of hope. It didn't matter that she'd been very quiet the rest of the day, keeping mostly to herself and sleeping most of the way home. He was depending on what had taken place that morning.

Could she be ignoring her subconscious emotions as he had? Reluctantly, he turned the key in the ignition. He wasn't going to get any answers by sitting there.

The next few days were going to be torture until he could see Jessie again. Maybe by then he could come up with some answers on how to win her.

"If I see you mooning over that damn rabbit one more time, I'll scream," Gina announced from behind Jessie. "You've been acting very strange ever since that little item arrived three days ago."

Jessie swung around in her chair to regard her friend. She grinned at her just to watch her grind her teeth. Even after three days of being pestered, she hadn't said a word to Gina about what had happened over the weekend. "What would you say if I told you that I think Trevor Planchet is a very nice man?"

"I'd consider sending you over to the state hospital for a thorough examination."

"Do I detect sour grapes?"

"I don't want him."

"I didn't mean that. I'd take you out, the best two out of three, if you did." She was truly enjoying herself. Too bad she didn't have something more substantial than a sleep-induced embrace to keep from her impetuous friend. "I meant you're just mad because I haven't given you a play-by-play of the weekend."

"Well, of course I am." Gina threw her hands up in the air, looking to the ceiling for deliverance. "I have to sit here day after day listening to you bitch and moan about the man chasing you for weeks. Then when he catches you, do you even tell me a single tantalizing detail? No. And you wonder why I'm frustrated."

"Nothing happened, at least not much," Jessie confessed as honestly as she could. Something had happened, but not what Gina wanted to know. Sometime during the weekend she had discovered that she could trust Trevor Planchet. Her instinct hadn't been far wrong that night at the theater. Beneath the façade of the clown was a nice man. A soft smile curved her lips as she remembered the evening by the campfire on the lake shore.

"What's not much?" Gina asked suspiciously.

"I thought you had to take the Devons' final plans to them this afternoon."

Her partner took a quick look at her watch and grimaced. "Not for another hour. Nice try, though. Are you going to tell me or not?"

"We had a nice platonic weekend. I'm sorry if that doesn't suit your trashy mind. The tabloids aren't going to make any money off of my personal life right now, so they'll have to concentrate on politicians and rock stars, as usual."

"How about later?"

"You don't ever give up, do you?" Jessie couldn't help but laugh at Gina's disgruntled expression before she walked back to her desk. She wanted the same answer. What was going to happen later? She had been disappointed Monday when she received Trevor's all too brief note. That night she'd felt a sense of relief when she watched the news, discovering exactly where he'd gone.

Would she have acted any differently on Sunday if she had known? That was a question that she asked herself time and time again. When Trevor wasn't in sight she could be brave and face up to her feelings. She turned into an emotional coward, however, the moment he appeared again. Though she no longer distrusted him, she wasn't sure about the extent of her feelings toward the man.

He was different from any man she had ever known. The other men she dated seemed dull and lifeless in comparison, but she had little or nothing in common with Trevor. Did it matter? Was it better for opposites to attract? Was she afraid that he would quickly grow tired of someone like her? Could she withstand the emotional ups and downs with someone like Trevor? The questions continued to circle around inside her head. Unfortunately, she couldn't discover an answer to a single one.

A few months ago her life had been mapped out, going exactly according to her plans. She had achieved all her goals. All her siblings had gotten their college degrees and her mother had settled in a nice retirement community. Her own college and training were behind her, and she'd opened her own business after long years of waiting. Then there had been the startling realization that she wanted a child, almost too late.

A new goal to be achieved, or so she had thought. Was it really a baby that she wanted, or did she want a person to fill up the empty corners of her life? It was yet another question in the circle. This one troubled her the most. When she had begun to seriously think about a baby, she had haunted the infants' departments at the local stores. She had wanted to be sure that that was what she wanted. After weeks of deliberating over the matter, she had made her decision: She would find a suitable husband and have a baby.

Had she been fooling herself all along? Trevor had shown her there was more to deciding on a husband than a list of qualifications. When she had composed her list, she had forgotten about the human factor. Until the Bushes' party, she'd been thinking about the man, the necessary father, as a two-dimensional figure, an essential ingredient that was needed to produce a child, but only as a catalyst. Maybe Gina was right about sperm bank roulette. Her own cold-blooded plan didn't seem much better.

How could a thirty-eight-year-old woman be so irrational about so many things? she wondered helplessly. Even when she was younger, she had known there were no easy solutions in the game of life. Maybe success in achieving her other goals had blinded her to reality. She had tried to put human relationships on the same level as earning a college diploma.

If she had married one of her candidates, she might have had her baby but quickly found herself in the divorce courts. She would have ended up like her mother as a single mother raising her child. Maybe having a baby wouldn't be so important if she had someone like Trevor in her life, a full-blooded, three-dimensional man to brighten her life. Or perhaps she was trying to rationalize all her motivations too much.

Only one thing seemed certain at the moment: She wanted Trevor to come home. He confused her, made her laugh, and he made her angry. One thing he didn't do was bore her. Only a week ago she never wanted to see him again, and now all she wanted was for him to walk through the door. It might not give her the answers she was seeking, but she knew it would make her happy.

"Hello, whoever this is. Let's make it quick," Trevor snapped into the phone. He'd been back in town for two hours and was just on his way out the back door to see Jessie before he reported to work. Nothing else was important. He should have left the answering machine on.

"Glad to have you back," Logan murmured dryly. "Have a nice trip?"

"Sorry, I'm a little preoccupied right now." He knew he was behaving like an adolescent, but he'd just had a miserable four days. He wanted to see Jessie in person after dreaming about her night after night.

"How many days has it been since you've seen Jessie?"

"Four days, twelve hours, and some odd minutes. Why, what's wrong?"

"Don't panic. I was just curious," Logan returned affably, his amusement clear over the phone line. "Got it really bad, haven't you?"

"Damn straight, so be careful of what you say," Trevor practically growled. Now he knew he had gone over the edge. He had panicked for a moment, thinking Logan was going to tell him that Jessie had gotten engaged or married while he was away. He was one huge mass of insecurity with a short fuse. "Did you want something, or did you just call to harass me now that your life is settled?"

"A little of both, but mostly it has to do with my happily settled life."

"Do you have to be so damn smug?"

"Probably. I called to ask you a favor, but now I've undoubtedly stuck my foot in it."

"It depends on the favor," Trevor replied, feeling a little more like himself as he taunted his sister's fiancé. "I'd be glad to run you over in the T-bird any time you'd like."

"You are in a good mood. Does that mean you won't be my best man at your sister's wedding?"

"Can I bring my shotgun?"

"I think your father's taking care of that," Logan stated with another chuckle. "He's threatened your rather frazzled sister with wearing his Confederate uniform to the wedding."

"Does he have one?" Trevor realized that he needed this nonsense to help him settle down. If he'd gone barreling into Jessie's office in the crazed condition he'd been in a few minutes ago, she would have thrown him out on his ear.

"I'm not sure if he has a uniform or not. We're not taking any chances, though. Arnette is checking all his closets,'' Logan explained quickly and earned a short laugh from Trevor. ''By the way, the rehearsal dinner is tonight and the wedding is Saturday.''

''What!?'' Trevor slumped against the kitchen cabinets, trying not to swear. After all, it was his little sister's wedding, but why now?

''You can bring a date, you know. It would be a good chance to introduce her to the rest of the family and get it over with. She should know what she's getting into by tangling with the Planchet clan.''

''Hey, you're right. You certainly don't waste any time, do you?'' He felt much better. Jessie couldn't object to going to a wedding. As he considered the matter, he decided it was ideal.

''It made sense to get married while I was still here on my assignment. Tory will have a chance to get her stores off the ground before our honeymoon and heading for Boston. Mother is already here, and considering Uncle Pres's illness, we thought we'd have the wedding while he could still enjoy the festivities. He and Babs flew in yesterday.''

''I'll bet he and T.L. have been making your lives miserable for the last twenty-four hours,'' Trevor chimed in as he remembered the two old friends together on a number of occasions over the years.

''Damn straight. According to them, they engineered the whole romance. Tory says you're to wear a dark suit and meet us at the house after your early broadcast, about seven-thirty. And to say hello to Jessie for her, too.''

Trevor hung up without saying good-bye. His sister was getting cute just because T.L. was on her case. Right now he had more important things to think about than sibling harassment. He'd take care of that later with Curtiss when they decorated the bride and groom's car tomorrow night.

* * *

"What, no baseball bunny?" Gina asked him as soon as he walked through the door of Aesthetics, Ltd. twenty minutes later. She was in the reception area gathering up tea cups and crumpled napkins. "I suppose those roses will do just as well."

"Hi, yourself," he answered, unsure of his welcome from her greeting. Jessie wasn't in sight, and he suddenly felt self-conscious with the flowers he clutched in his hand. It was a first for him, he decided, never having experienced the emotion before.

"You got me in trouble, you know. Jessie wasn't terribly pleased that I gave you the list," she stated heatedly, placing one hand on her hip as if waiting for his explanation. "Couldn't you have kept it to yourself? It could have been our little secret."

"Sorry, it sort of slipped out in the heat of the moment," he admitted, remembering his stupidity that afternoon at his house. He became irrational when Jessie was in his arms.

"That sounds more promising than anything that she's been telling me." The brunette seemed to perk up at his admission.

"Nope, you're not getting anything out of me, either." He held up his free hand in the semblance of a pledge.

"If I'm not going to get any good gossip out of you, I guess I might as well let you talk to Jessie.

"You mean she's here?"

"She is now," Gina announced as he spun around in time to see Jessie walk through the door. "She went downstairs to get some copies made."

Trevor almost threw all caution to the wind at the sight of her. Her silky black hair was down around her shoulders, windswept and beautiful. The filmy dress she wore was a riot of colors and clung to every sweet curve. But it was her smile that was almost his undoing. Her delicate features lit up with pleasure at the sight of him.

"Hi." That was all he could manage around the constriction in his throat. His dreams had been accurate. How could he forget how beautiful she was in only four days?"

"Trevor." She stopped just inside the door, as if she wasn't sure he was real.

"You two need some serious help," Gina said dryly. Walking to Trevor's side, she grabbed his arm and shook it. "Are you going to give her the flowers, or what?"

"Gina!" Jessie came out of her trance to chastise her friend.

"Hey, it's a dirty job, but somebody had to do it," the brunette returned, giving a careless shrug. "Since I think this is going to be too painful to watch, I'm going to be in the storeroom until he leaves."

"I may not tell you," Jessie called after her.

"I'll take that chance," Gina remarked as she walked out of sight.

"I'm not sure she likes me anymore." Trevor looked over his shoulder toward the back of the office.

"The trouble all along has been that she likes you just fine," Jessie answered, but her gentle smile took any sting out of the words.

"These are for you, in case you were wondering." He felt like a kid on prom night giving out his first corsage.

"Thank you, they're beautiful." She took the bouquet from him and gathered it to her face to inhale the fragrance of the twelve blooms.

"Gina thought maybe you'd rather have another rabbit," Trevor commented as she placed the roses carefully in the cut-glass vase on the coffee table.

"And she thinks I'm the crazy one," Jessie murmured, turning quickly to face him again. She clasped her hands in front of her like a little girl waiting for a special treat. "When did you get back?"

"Just over two hours ago." He didn't mind telling her that he'd made her his first priority. "I have to check in at work soon, but I wanted to ask you something first. I know it's short notice—" He broke off, wondering how he was going to phrase this. Logan said taking Jessie to the rehearsal dinner and wedding was a good idea, but now he wasn't so sure.

"Trevor?"

He knew it was now or never. If she didn't want to have anything to do with him, she would refuse. "Would you like to go to dinner tonight?"

"What time?" Her smile was back in place, but maybe she was just being polite.

"I'll pick you up a little after seven, when I get done at the station." He held his breath, anticipating and dreading her answer at the same time.

"That sounds fine. I have a meeting at five-thirty, but it shouldn't be too long," she replied in a rush of words, almost as if she'd been holding her breath until that moment. "What should I wear?"

"Something dressy, I guess. I don't know much about these things, but that sounds safe," he said, wondering offhand if there was a standard dress for rehearsal dinners. He glanced at his watch and realized that he had to leave. "Look I've got to get to work, so I'll see you around seven."

"Fine."

For a moment he simply stood drinking in the sight of her. That would have to last him over the next six hours. There was something else he wanted to do and wondered if he dared. In a split second, he threw all caution to the wind and took a step forward. The moment he touched her he knew that he wasn't going to make a fool out of himself. Jessie came willingly into his arms.

She tasted as sweet and intoxicating as he had remembered. Like a potent wine, her kisses went quickly to his head. He didn't dare deepen the kiss. The feel of Jessie's hands gliding over his shirt was hazardous enough to his self-control. Drawing away reluctantly, he looked down into her luminous blue eyes.

"See you tonight, sweetheart," he managed, then turned away before he forgot his job, his family, and the rest of the world except Jessica DeLord.

TEN

As they drove through the Heights, Jessie began to wonder where they were going to dinner. There were dozens of restaurants in the commercial districts along the bluffs that rose above the Arkansas River, but she didn't know of any in the residential area where Trevor had turned off a few minutes before.

"When are you going to tell me where we're going?" she asked finally, completely lost from the twists and turns he'd been making. He'd been remarkably subdued since he'd picked her up fifteen minutes earlier. In the fading light of dusk, she wondered if she was imagining his uncertain attitude. "Trevor?"

"Will you promise to go out with me tomorrow if I tell you where we're going?"

She gave him a curious look, trying to figure out why he would sound nervous. When he pulled the car to the side of the road, she was more than curious. "Are you resorting to blackmail now?"

"Will it work?" He hooked his arm along the back of the seat, heightening her awareness of the close confines of the small two-seater car.

"I'm not sure. If today were my birthday, I might

be suspicious about all this mysterious behavior. But my birthday isn't until September, so you and Gina couldnt've hatched some crazy plot.'' She searched his face for some sign of humor. Trevor was still looking uneasy. ''Is it really that bad?''

''You'll have to tell me after you meet the rest of my family,'' he answered slowly, his fingers reaching up to play with the strands of hair that fell to the shoulder of her burgundy silk dress. ''Of course, you've met Sanders, so his wife, Curtiss, Leeanne, and all the kids shouldn't be too much of a shock.''

''We're going to have dinner with your family?'' She measured every word, almost giving in to the temptation of jumping out of the car. It certainly wasn't what she had expected.

''This is the last place I ever imagined taking you, but my sister managed to blow all my plans sky high,'' he explained, giving her a spaniel look that tugged at her heart. ''Logan caught me just as I was leaving the house. He and Tory are getting married tomorrow, and I'm going to be the best man. Instead of taking you to the intimate little Italian place I had in mind, we're going to my sister's rehearsal dinner.''

''Oh, boy.'' That was all she could manage. She'd run around all afternoon like a hyperactive teenager worrying about her first real date with Trevor. What should she say? How should she act? Was she behaving rationally? Her bedroom looked like a tornado had struck. Nothing she owned suited her; nothing was going to be right for dinner with Trevor. After five changes, she'd settled on a plain but stylish burgundy sheath moments before he had arrived. If she had known the truth, she might have been twice as nervous.

''It really won't be that bad, Jessie. I promise.'' His

hand dropped to her shoulder to give a reassuring squeeze before he put the car in gear again.

A few minutes later, when the imposing gates came into view, Jessie wondered if she shouldn't have told him to take her home. The sight of the house a few minutes later, however, changed her mind. The view of the twin Queen Anne turrets against the last remnants of the sunset took her breath away. She had had no idea this gem of a house was hidden away in the modern suburbs of Little Rock. Apparently T.L. wanted his home to be a well-kept secret. She couldn't remember ever seeing pictures of it in any of the local or regional magazines.

"Here we are. The old homestead." Trevor let out a deep breath as he turned off the ignition.

"It's beautiful," Jessie exclaimed, not waiting for him to help her out of the car. She wanted an unobstructed view of the house, momentarily forgetting her anxiety.

"Don't say I didn't warn you about Daddy's taste in furniture," he murmured as he took her arm and led her up the back steps and through the heart-shaped moon gate entrance to the porch.

When they entered the house, they could hear the rumble of voices coming from the front rooms. Just as they reached the kitchen door, Arnette stepped into the hall, a tray of hors d'oeuvres in her hands. "It's about time you got here. I've had to set dinner back a half hour already." Her face broke into a smile when she saw Jessie. "Now, didn't I tell you she was a nice girl? It's so nice to see you again, Miss DeLord. Maybe this boy has more sense than I gave him credit for all this time."

"Trevor, dammit. How could you?" another voice broke in from the far end of the hall while Jessie was returning Arnette's greeting.

"How could I what?" he asked cautiously, giving Jessie a sidelong glance before he turned back to Abby Bush, who was rapidly walking toward them.

"I told you that Jessie was too nice for you, didn't I? I can't believe that you had the nerve to ask her out after what you did at my party," she stated with great heat before turning to Jessie. "I'm so sorry about this menace. I meant to call and warn you not to trust him in a well-lit room with an empty gun."

"I don't think he's that bad." Jessie was beginning to relax at the two women's affectionate teasing. She thought Trevor was a little too complacent after the dual attack. "You can't be as bad as people say you are. Can you?"

"Maybe I should have taken you back home when I had the chance," he grumbled good-naturedly, grasping Jessie's arm and linking it through his. "Heel, Abby. She's safe as long as she's under your watchful eye. Although I'm beginning to suspect a setup."

"A setup?" Jessie asked. At the suddenly guilty look on Abby's face, Jessie decided that she must be missing a piece of information.

"Unless I miss my guess, I think my sister and this young lady were going to try their delicate little hands at some reverse-psychology matchmatching," he explained, a satisfied smirk on his face as Abby began to sputter in outrage. "It seems that you and I were going to be victims of a horrible plot. Only I scotched their devious plans by having the excellent taste of staking my claim first."

Jessie looked from Abby to Trevor, trying to make sense of the exchange. Suddenly the pieces fell into place. Abby Bush's warnings to Trevor were supposed to pique his interest in Jessie. It was too ironic for words. Abby would never know that at that point of their acquaintance Trevor scared Jessie spitless. Now, though still wary of the man, she couldn't help joining in the fun. "Abby, you didn't purposely introduce me to Connor MacMurray simply to make Trevor look good in comparison?"

"Oh, Lord, he's corrupted you already," she wailed dramatically, playing her part to the hilt, but having a tough time keeping a straight face. "No, I didn't, but for that comment I'm glad I put you two at the kiddie table for dinner."

"Hey, are y'all going to stand out there all night?" T.L.'s voice boomed out from a distant room. "The minister hasn't got all night, boy. So get your sorry behind in here."

"Just one man's family," Trevor murmured dryly, leading Jessie toward the front of the house. "Why did I think this was a good idea? I'm going to make Logan pay for this one. That cowardly Yankee doesn't want a best man; he just wants reinforcements to help deal with these lunatics."

"Trevor, are you all right? I think you're babbling." Jessie tried to contain her laughter, but with little success. She understood now why the man beside her didn't hesitate to act outrageously whenever the spirit moved him. He was surrounded by people who weren't afraid to speak their minds, no matter where they were. It was a talent he had acquired for self-defense.

He stopped just before they reached the entrance to the living room, placing his hands on her shoulders. Looking very earnest and keeping his voice low, he said, "I apologize ahead of time for anything that happens here tonight, Jessie. Things are already out of control, and we've only been in the house for five minutes."

"Trevor, I'm enjoying myself," she returned just as solemnly, touched by his obvious distress. With a daring she didn't quite understand, she leaned forward and kissed his cheek. "Why don't you relax? If I didn't know better, I'd think this was your wedding rehearsal."

That seemed to subdue him for the next half hour as he introduced her to the members of his family and Logan Herrington's. Abby, as Tory's matron of honor, and her husband were the only others present who weren't related to the bride and groom.

The rest of the evening continued with a great deal of boisterous laughter and affectionate teasing. The only ones who didn't join in the general mayhem were Sanders and his family. Jessie almost went into a fit of giggles when she met little Basil, wishing Gina could have been with her at that moment. The poor child was the spitting image of his stodgy father. She almost hugged Trevor for coming into her life before she had selected one of her candidates and ended up with someone like Sanders.

It was soon apparent that Tory's sense of humor was almost as bizarre as her brother's. She also bore the brunt of most of the ribbing, especially from Trevor and Curtiss, the soft-spoken veterinarian. Logan joined in at one point, recounting how Tory had decided to teach him to be a laid-back Southerner. His aunt and uncle had been in tears from laughing over the matter, and his mother, the epitome of a Bostonian grand dame, smiled occasionally.

Jessie was almost sorry when Trevor declared that it was time to leave. They were delayed as Ty Daniel and Amanda Sue demanded that their uncle tell them one more story before he left. At six and three, the two urchins had held court at the kiddie table all through dinner, their uncle their willing slave. He gave in with very little resistance, recounting a story about a beautiful raven-haired princess who refused to be courted by her father's jester.

Trying to look disinterested as Trevor told the tale

with his dancing eyes trained directly on her, Jessie was ready to leave as soon as the children gave their uncle his good-night kisses. The two tow-headed children also graciously included Jessie in the ceremony, much to the delight of all the adults. They had listened carefully to Trevor's story as well.

As she settled into the passenger seat, Jessie felt her earlier nervousness beginning to return. The evening had been wonderful, a sharp contrast to spending time with her own family. Though she had a large family, they were quiet, reserved people who didn't show their emotions readily. For a moment, she wondered what would happen if she mixed the two families together. She wasn't quite sure.

"Are you ever going to speak to me again?" Trevor asked a few minutes later, breaking the companionable silence in the car.

"Because of your family or that absurd story you told the children?" she asked quickly, trying to read his thoughts as she gazed at his profile. A sudden thought occurred to her. "Did Tory really break your nose? I thought it must be a football injury."

"That's the trouble with families, they don't allow you any secrets." His grumbling had the same mock ferociousness he had used when weaving the fairy tale for his niece and nephew.

"It certainly gave me a new perspective," she returned quietly. He didn't answer immediately, deliberating over her comment.

"Is that good or bad?"

She waited for a few moments, seriously considering the matter. Though she hadn't the time to assess everything she'd heard and seen, she had learned a great deal about Trevor Planchet. "I'd say it was good."

He didn't answer as he turned the car into her driveway. Though he switched off the engine, he made no move to get out of the car. Jessie wondered what was going on in his fertile brain. The one thing she knew by now was that she couldn't anticipate what he would do next. He proved her right when he finally spoke.

"I'm not going to walk you to the door, Jessie." He said the words very slowly and clearly, as if he were making a proclamation.

"I see." She didn't, but with one look at his still form beside her, she didn't think she wanted to question his reasons. He was staring straight ahead through the windshield, his entire body poker stiff with his arms straining against the steering wheel.

"I don't think you do." He turned to face her, his hands still gripping the steering wheel tightly. "All I want to do right now is carry you into the house and make love to you all night long until we're both exhausted. In my present state of mind, I don't think we'd make it much farther than the front door."

She didn't know what to say. He'd taken her breath away. Tiny sparks seemed to be traveling through her bloodstream. All too clearly she could remember the morning in the camping shelter. She closed her eyes for a moment, almost considering telling him that she understood exactly what he was feeling. He didn't give her a chance.

"The only thing that's holding me back is the fact that I don't think you're ready to take that step yet," he continued, his voice suddenly rough as he watched her expression in the dim light from the dashboard. "Tonight's only a beginning, sweetheart. Now go inside before I forget that I have some principles."

For a moment she hesitated, wanting to throw her arms around his neck and tell him what an incredibly considerate man he was. He had always told her he wasn't as dangerous as she thought. Now she believed him.

"Jessie."

At his harsh growl, she grabbed the door handle and scrambled out of the car. She ran up the walk to the front door to keep from turning around and getting back into the car. As she inserted the key into the lock, her mind told her that he was right. Unfortunately, the traitorous little voice was telling her what her body wanted. She ached to feel his arms around her again, to taste the magic of his kiss and explore all the secrets of his lean body.

Opening the door, she turned to watch Trevor's car slowly back out of the drive. She knew she had a sleepless night ahead, even if she was spending it alone. The evening had taught her quite a few things about the complex man who had just sent her off to bed alone. Myriad questions continued to circle in her bewildered mind. Some of them now had answers, but a thousand more seemed to take their place.

One thing she knew for certain, it would take her a lifetime to understand Trevor Planchet.

"You've been awfully quiet," Trevor commented as he guided Jessie between the other dancers on the special flooring of the pavilion erected on the Planchet's lawn. "Or is my family finally getting to you? Maybe the two hundred intimate friends that Daddy invited in for drinks and a snack?"

Victoria Planchet's wedding to Logan Herrington had become an event, in spite of the couple's protests. The wedding had been small and elegant, performed in her father's living room with only thirty witnesses present. The bride was lovely in a white silk suit complemented by a large white hat, and the groom had looked solemn in a pearl-gray suit as they had exchanged their vows. T.L., however, had taken it upon himself to orchestrate the reception in his own style.

Most of Little Rock's prominent citizens were now drinking pink champagne from a fountain set up in the gazebo or dancing to the full orchestra that played beneath the canopy of the trees. The Langford-Hugheses were among the first to arrive. The bride and groom were oblivious to most of the guests, dancing together in their own world. T.L. was in his element, playing the convivial host for all he was worth.

"Your father is certainly a law unto himself," Jessie returned quietly, unable to tell Trevor what was on her mind. She was still unsettled by the revelation she had experienced only a half hour ago. Right now she wanted to hug her new knowledge to herself.

"Yes, and I think he's lucky that Tory can only think about Logan today. If not, I wouldn't want to be in his shoes. He had her biggest competitor cater the damn thing." Trevor chuckled as he watched his father giving the waiters instruction on exactly where to put the wedding cake. "I'm thinking about eloping myself, just to frustrate the old man. Now that I'm the only one of his children who's single, he'll probably want to hire Ringling Brothers to entertain at my wedding."

Trevor's wedding was the last thing that Jessie wanted to talk about at that particular moment. After weeks of conflicting emotions and noble statements about the ideal husband, she suddenly realized half an hour ago that she was in love with the impossible man. True to form, it had been when he'd been doing something absurd.

He'd been standing next to Logan, his demeanor quiet and seeming extremely dignified in his charcoal-gray suit. Jessie had thought he looked absolutely wonderful from her seat next to Gary Bush. Then Trevor had looked straight at her, giving her a leering wink. Her heart had stopped for a half second, and she couldn't breathe. Instantaneously, and as unexpected as the man himself, came the realization that she loved him.

When the wedding march began a few minutes later, she wasn't sure she could stand up. But as she rose hesitantly to her feet, the idea took hold, and she wanted to laugh out loud. It was probably inevitable from the moment she'd turned to find a half-naked six-foot rabbit standing by her side. She was the only one who didn't suspect it would happen. Abby, Tory, and Gina had all seemed to think it was an ideal match.

What did Trevor think? she wondered as she gazed up at his smiling face. He seemed to want a relationship, but what kind? As he had said, he was the only Planchet who wasn't married. The big question was why he wasn't?

"Jessie, you're not mad about last night, are you?"

She looked up at him in confusion. "I told you I enjoyed being with your family, and I had a delightful evening."

"That's not what I was talking about," he informed her, his expression almost as solemn as it had been during Tory's wedding.

"Oh." He meant when he had taken her home. The vulnerable expression in his dark eyes took her by surprise. Was he really that worried about what he'd done? Didn't he realize that was one of the reasons she had fallen in love with him? "No, of course, I'm not mad. Why would I be?"

"You could think— Never mind, let's dance." He slipped both arms around her waist, holding her close as he led her into a slow, dreamy rhythm.

Jessie circled her arms around his neck and nestled her head against his shoulder. She gave herself up to the movement of his lean body against hers. Would he tell her to run for the sake of her virtue again tonight?

He might be that noble, she decided judiciously, but she wasn't.

The traitorous little voice inside her was giving her all sorts of wicked suggestions, and they all included the very delectable body of Trevor Planchet. Every single suggestion seemed perfect. For once she thought she might be able to surprise him. It was time that she took some control, instead of letting Trevor direct their relationship.

With a daring she didn't know she possessed, Jessie began to make her plans for the evening. She needed to start behaving like a mature woman who made her own decisions and guided her own destiny again.

"Trevor, why haven't you gotten married?" She timed the question exactly a mile and a half from her house, just to test the waters before she went in for the kill.

"What kind of question is that?" he demanded, taking his eyes off the road momentarily. "Is this one of those women things after attending a wedding?"

"You said something earlier about being the last one to be single in your family. Of course, you forgot about your father," she answered in an offhand tone. For good measure, she looked idly out the window. "If you're just counting your brothers and sister, you're not the baby of the family or anything. At least I don't think you are. How old are you?"

"That's not a ladylike question," he returned quickly, giving her another quizzical look at the non sequitur. "You've been in a strange mood all afternoon. Is there something wrong?"

"No, you impossible man. Now, are you going to answer my questions?" She turned, purposely hiking up her skirt as she casually curled her legs up onto the seat. Draping one arm over the back of the bench seat, she leaned her head against his shoulder. Did he notice that she'd moved closer?''

"Probably the same reason you haven't gotten married by now," he said abruptly, overly preoccupied with steering the car down the quiet residential street.

"What reason is that?" she murmured, trailing her fingers under the collar of his pale blue shirt, then moving on to the knot of his striped tie.

"I've been too busy with my job and life in general." He was stoically trying to ignore her wandering fingers, showing Jessie that she had a lot of work ahead of her. Trevor was set on being noble again tonight.

"Is that all?" As she traced the shell of his ear with her index finger, she realized that she was having fun. She could understand why Trevor and his family ignored most of their inhibitions and the usual social conventions, even if it seemed outrageous to anyone watching. It was a liberating experience. Why hadn't she realized this before?

"I suppose so. There's the old line about the time, the place, and the loved one, which probably has something to do with it," he said, still preoccupied with his driving as he turned the car into her driveway. When he shifted into park, Jessie reached over and turned off the ignition. For good measure she took possession of the keys, dropping them on the floor behind her.

Trevor seemed dumbfounded by her actions, staring at the empty ignition as if it might explode any minute. Slowly he cocked his head to the side and sat very still as he regarded her. His face was in shadows, so she couldn't see his expression. Why was he so still?

"Sweet heaven, Jessie, I hope you know what you're doing," he finally gritted out through clenched teeth. She could feel the tension in his cheek as she traced the line of his jaw with the back of her hand.

"I think so. I was awfully lonely after you left last

night," she murmured, taking the opportunity to move closer until her shoulder brushed against his. If she moved another inch she would be in his lap. "I think I had a deprived adolescence. Do you know that I've never necked in a parked car?"

"Oh, Jessie," he groaned.

She never saw him move, but a moment later she was draped across his lap with the steering wheel pressing against her back. A giggle bubbled up in her throat when she looked up into his scowling face.

"By rights I should turn you over my knee for spoiling all my good intentions," he grumbled, but she could see that he was having trouble maintaining his glower.

"Couldn't we try it straight first before you get kinky?" she asked sweetly, running her hands up the front of his shirt. Without waiting for an answer she began working on the knot of his tie.

"Jessie . . ." His voice was a cross between a command and a plea this time.

"You keep saying that," she murmured, noting that his hand was moving in a slow circle on her thigh. His show of resistance was beginning to crumble, bit by bit. The pressure of his arousal was noticeably increasing against her hip. "Aren't you going to do anything else?"

"I want you to be sure that you know what you're doing," he said earnestly, still not making an overt move to either help or reject her. "There's no turning back after this, sweetheart."

She didn't answer with words. Instead, she languidly unbuttoned his shirt. In a very deliberate movement, she leaned forward, running her palms over taut, hair-roughened skin until she linked her hands behind his head. Brazenly she rubbed her breasts against him, and when her lips were a mere millimeter from his, she whispered, "Oh, Trevor."

That was all it took to snap his control. His arms closed roughly around her as he groaned her name once more. For a moment, Jessie wondered what she had unleashed, but when his mouth claimed hers she didn't care.

It wasn't a tentative, gentle first embrace. Trevor had been tormented beyond his limit, and was intent on slaking the hunger she had aroused in him. His hands moved over her awkwardly, seemingly unable to find a resting place, but Jessie was in the throes of the same spell. She couldn't get close enough, twisting and turning in his arms as she battled his tongue for possession of the dark, mysterious depths of their fervent kisses.

"Sweet heaven, Jessie, what are we doing?" Trevor finally gasped, the sound of ripping material bringing him back to his senses. He dropped his head back against the seat, staring at the ceiling of the car while he tried to control his labored breathing.

Jessie sagged against him, laying her head against his shoulder. She was dazed and extremely happy about what had just taken place. Trevor's hand stroked her damp hair soothingly. "I think we were ravaging each other," she said. "Is that what you were talking about last night?"

"Jessie, what has gotten into you?" he asked in wonder, not bothering to move.

"Nothing yet. I think that's the problem," she answered wickedly, biting her lower lip in anticipation of his response.

"Dammit, Jessie, warn me when you're going to say something like that," he almost growled, swooping down to press a hard kiss on her bare shoulder. For a moment, she wondered how her dress had come partially off before Trevor said, "I think my heart stopped for a minute."

"It feels like it's going strong to me." She placed her hand over the organ in question, moving her palm against his damp skin in a widening circle. Almost immediately Trevor's hand clamped around her wrist, holding her in place. With his other hand he pulled her dress back up over her shoulder.

"We're going to have to get dressed just to get out of the car," he announced, sounding almost as dazed as she felt a few moments before. "Jessie, I don't think I've ever lost control like that in my entire life. We've even managed to steam up the windows."

"Isn't it wonderful?" She reached up to kiss him again, but he forestalled her with a firm grip on her shoulders.

"No more of this until we get into the house," he said firmly.

"Promise?" Jessie looked directly into his eyes, trying to read his expression in the dim light.

"I promise. Now, what the hell did you do with my keys?"

Jessie kept giggling and Trevor swore, which made her laugh even harder, as they worked at untangling themselves to search for the keys. Fifteen minutes later, as they walked to the front door, Jessie slipped her arm around Trevor's waist. With gratifying promptness, he curved an arm around her shoulder. Once inside, however, he seemed to hesitate again.

"Trevor?" She wasn't sure she liked the almost haunted look on his face. Dropping her shoes on the carpet, she took his hand to lead him toward the bedroom. He stayed firmly in place. "What is it?"

"I have something to tell you."

The bubble inside her seemed to fizzle and die under his hooded gaze. She couldn't tell what he was thinking. Was he having second thoughts about what happened in the car? "Is it important?"

"I think it's damned important," he shot back, his frown deepening as he studied her face. "You've got me so confused that I don't know what's happening anymore."

"Are you going to renege on your promise?" she asked, trying to put off what he was going to say. She was sure she wasn't going to like it.

"Dammit, Jessie, I'm trying to tell you that I love you, and all you can think about is sex," he snapped, then realized what he had just said.

Jessie knew her mouth was hanging open, but she couldn't help it. The man continually surprised her. She said the first thing that came to her mind. "Well, how was I supposed to know? I only figured out I loved you this afternoon."

The silence in the entryway was deafening. Neither one of them seemed to know what to do or say next. Trevor managed to recover first, stepping forward and swinging Jessie up into his arms. He didn't speak but strode purposefully toward the back of the house.

"I guess this means you're going to keep your promise after all," she said impishly, raining butterfly kisses on his face.

"Damn straight."

"You're such a romantic, Trevor Planchet," she murmured, nipping at his ear. "The bedroom's the second door on the left."

"I thought we'd get comfortable before we continued the discussion," he returned with a wry twist to his mouth as he set her on her feet next to the bed. "I'm kind of curious about how my princess turned into a sex kitten all of a sudden."

Jessie grinned, pleased by his description that undoubtedly would have horrified her weeks ago. Sliding his suit jacket off his shoulders, she explained, "I think Abby was right and you've corrupted me. A few days ago I realized I needed a flesh-and-blood man, not some two-dimensional shadow to be the father of my child. Then it took a little while to admit it was you."

"This baby thing is something else we need to discuss."

"Later, much later. Right now I want to talk about us," she said gently, beginning to unbutton his shirt again.

"You decided that I wasn't anything like your father," he guessed accurately while his hand worked on the zipper of her dress. "A lot of things began to fall into place after you told me about your family. I probably came across as an idiot when I first met you."

"A little, but a very sexy idiot. I've always thought of myself as very staid and serious, so I couldn't imagine any reason for someone like you to be interested in me. You just kept showing up." She dropped his shirt on the floor and gave a satisfied sigh as she ran her hand over his chest. "You scared me to death, but I kept remembering how delicious you looked in your rabbit outfit."

" 'Delicious'?" Trevor looked a little embarrassed by the word, although it didn't stop his clever fingers from unhooking the clasp of Jessie's lace bra. "I think that applies to you in that little red number you had on at the Bushes' party. Want to wear it for me again sometime?"

"Are we getting kinky again?"

"I think you mentioned we should do it straight first," he murmured, his hands slipping beneath the layers of her satin panties and pantyhose to pull her close into the heat of his desire.

Together they finished undressing and slipped onto the bed in a tender embrace. Jessie was amazed at his gentleness as he set out to explore her body slowly. They had the confidence of new lovers, secure in their feelings. They knew they had all the time in the world, stroking and caressing each other as if neither of them had experienced lovemaking before. She sighed as his fingers teased the slope of her breast before his lips softly sipped at the hardened peak. He murmured his approval as she alternately kneaded and caressed his chest and hips.

Time seemed to stand still, transporting them to a place all their own. This time Jessie felt the heat begin to kindle within her ever so slowly, almost like her dream while they were camping. She knew it was more than a dream now as Trevor captured her lips in a leisurely, soulful kiss that seemed to pledge his devotion. Pulling him close into the cradle of her hips, she returned his pledge with a promise of her own.

Suddenly the lassitude seemed to leave them both, and the storm of passion that had taken them earlier quickly returned. Trevor groaned as she wrapped her legs around him, urging him on. After running from him for so long, she wanted to show him how much she truly cared. Arching up to meet his driving thrusts, she fleetingly wondered what kind of child they would make. Then as completion claimed them both, she knew that she would be content with only Trevor in her life.

ELEVEN

"Trevor, wake up. It's time for me to go to work." Jessie looked down fondly at his sleeping face where he lay using her breast as a pillow. Even after twenty-four hours, she wasn't sure that she wasn't in a dream. They had barely moved from her bedroom yesterday, only foraging in the kitchen to satisfy their more mundane appetites. For hours they talked about the chaotic weeks behind them and their plans for the future. They made slow, leisurely love, reveling in the freedom to express themselves physically and emotionally.

Now reality was disrupting their paradise in the form of her alarm clock. She had to get to work, and Trevor was a dead weight that kept her from moving. "Trevor, get up."

"Justhitthesnooze," he grumbled as his hand came up to fondle her breast. A silly smile curved his lips.

"Oh, no, you don't." She pinched his shoulder before he could undermine her resolve. After all, most of her busy schedule this week was working on his house.

"Hey, that hurt. This doesn't bode well for our future together," he muttered, but only moved over to clutch the pillow next to her.

"I've got to get to the office to check on your deliveries, buster," she explained and bent to placate him with a kiss. She made sure she kept a close eye on his hands, however. It wasn't necessary, since he was already asleep. With a philosophical shrug, she headed for the shower.

A half hour later she returned to the bedroom, fully dressed and with a cup of hot tea in her hand. Trevor hadn't moved. Was she going to be able to have a coherent conversation with him before she left?

Just then his arm reached out, and when he found only empty space, he opened his eyes. He looked at her upright figure balefully. Then he pushed himself up on his elbows and shook his entire body like a wet dog.

Jessie watched in rapt fascination. "Do you do that every morning?"

"Only when I find gorgeous women in my room." Flipping over, he punched up the pillows behind him and leaned back.

"It better be only one woman from now on, especially in my house." She softened her words by sitting down on the edge of the bed to kiss him.

"Mmmm, maybe I could get up at this unholy hour if that's my reward," he murmured a few minutes later. "Sure you don't want to stay home and try to make babies?"

"I knew I never should have told you why I was looking for a husband. I'm never going to live it down."

"Are you always this alert as soon as you get up?" he asked suspiciously, scrubbing the palms of his hands over his face. "We're going to have some serious trouble ahead, since I'm barely coherent before noon."

"Just something else we can work out together." She started to get up, but his hand at her wrist kept her in place. "I have a feeling we're going to have a very educational period of adjustment."

"Jessie, how serious are you about having a baby?" he asked earnestly, apparently making an effort to be awake.

She considered the question as she sipped her tea, not coming up with an easy answer. "I don't know. I thought a baby was what I wanted, but I'm not sure I wasn't simply looking for someone like you. Someone to share my life with."

"That's what you've got, but I don't want you to give up on something you really want," he stated firmly. He became engrossed in watching the movement of his thumb moving over the back of her hand. "My house is definitely big enough for kids, so there isn't any reason to put off getting married. I remember reading about women having babies later in life, and it gets more difficult after forty."

"Married?" Jessie almost spilled her tea on his bare chest.

"You were planning on marrying me, weren't you?" Trevor looked provoked by her surprise.

"I hadn't gotten that far. I'm still trying to adjust to waking up in your arms," she answered honestly. "Do you want to get married?"

"Damn straight. I didn't go to all the trouble of chasing you for a silly affair."

"Okay, don't get angry. Saturday night was the first time I've ever seduced someone, and now we're talking marriage. I'm just not used to any of this." She smiled at him to ask his forgiveness, trying to ignore the rapid beating of her heart. Trevor wanted to marry her.

"Get used to this." He snaked his hand around her neck and pulled down her head, claiming her mouth with his. For a moment he teased her by nibbling on her lower lip, then suddenly deepened the kiss, plundering and taking a heated response.

"Oh, boy. I'm not going to get anything done for the rest of the day," she managed to gasp a few minutes later. Getting unsteadily to her feet, she belatedly remembered her cup on the nightstand. "I'll see you tonight."

"I'll be doing the late show, so just wait for me in bed," he told her, wiggling his eyebrows suggestively.

Jessie hurried out of the room before she changed her mind and climbed back into bed. She'd known all along that Trevor Planchet was going to be a bad influence in her life, only she hadn't realized how much she was going to enjoy it.

"The turret room would be a great room for a little girl, wouldn't it?"

Jessie murmured sleepily in response, not really registering the words that rumbled in her ear. She was too comfortable snuggled against Trevor's warm body. The past three days had been absolute heaven, she decided in drowsy satisfaction, idly stroking the hair-roughened plane of her lover's chest.

"Stop that. I'm trying to have a serious discussion," he ordered, but softened the reprimand by capturing her hand and raising it to his lips.

"What did you want to discuss?" She tilted her head back to look up into his solemn face. The sight of him in the moonlight was still too new for her not to marvel at her luck. Her fantasies about Trevor's brass bed had exceeded her expectations. "I thought you'd be tired after working late tonight."

"Do you want a boy or a girl?"

"You're becoming obsessed with this." With a sigh, she placed her palms on his chest, resting her chin on them as she met his gaze. Children seemed to be a

subject he returned to again and again. "We haven'
even discussed the wedding yet, and you want to talk
about children."

"Well, the Planchets seem to run to boys, but I think
a little girl with black hair and blue eyes would be
perfect." His fingers tangling in her hair made her want
to purr, but she was beginning to know his moods. He
wanted to be serious, at least for the next few minutes
"Men have biological time clocks, too."

"I just focused on finding a husband, then having a
healthy baby, and never really thought about whether
it would be a boy or a girl," she admitted. "I have an
equal number of nieces and nephews, though only six
of my brothers and sisters are married. Mother and
Aunt Lena are working hard to get Phillip and Cassie
down the aisle, though."

"I'm not sure I'll ever remember all of them. It will
take a score card to keep them straight," he murmured
his gaze thoughtful. "Maybe I wasn't kidding about the
Ringling Brothers at my wedding. Your family will be
quite a crowd. Tell me the roster again."

"My family is not a football team," she protested
good-naturedly. She'd had twenty-six years to get used
to the number, but having that many prospective in
laws probably was a little daunting. "Okay, here we go
You talked to my mother, Aunt Lena, and Betsy two
days ago when we officially announced our engagement."

"Right. Your mother lives in Florida with your Aunt
Lena. Betsy is the next oldest and runs a souvenir shop
with her husband in Branson, Missouri." He smiled in
triumph at his recitation, then frowned as he tried to
remember the rest. "You and Betsy went to college
together, because you all took turns going to school
and working part-time to help each other with tuition
She has four kids, and two of them are twins?"

"No, Julie and Janet are twins, and Betsy has two

little girls. I think I'd better do this by age." She couldn't help giggling over his confusion. Except for the night they'd shared childhood reminiscences by the campfire, she hadn't discussed her family. "I'm the oldest—"

"And the prettiest."

"Thank you," she acknowledged graciously, dropping a kiss on his collarbone.

"None of that. We have important matters to discuss."

"Spoil sport. Betsy is a year younger, Cameron and Miles are a year younger than she is; Cam still lives in the old homestead outside Jackson with his wife and two boys. Miles is a forest ranger in South Dakota. Julie and Janet come next; they're the twins. They are both married and each has two girls." She paused for a minute to check if Trevor was still awake. He had one arm propped behind his head, and though his forehead was creased in concentration, his eyes were closed.

"Hey, why'd you stop?"

"Just checking to see if you were keeping up."

"We were on the twins," he prompted before settling back in place. His free hand stroked absently up and down her bare back, but his mind was preoccupied with her family.

"After the twins are Lawrence and Duncan. The four of them liked working in Mom and Aunt Lena's bake shop when they were growing up and went into business together after college. They've expanded and have three stores in Jackson and four in Memphis."

"Any kids?"

"You *are* obsessed." She really didn't mind. Their whispered conversations in the middle of the night were something she was coming to cherish. Once she had finished her litany, she was sure she could channel his thoughts in another direction.

"No, I want to get this right."

"Maybe I should get you a pencil and paper," she returned dryly at his earnest tone.

"Just keep going. I think I'm finally getting them all straight."

"Larry has a little girl and Duncan has a son. That leaves Phillip and Cassie—the two babies, as the parents insist on calling them, even if both of them are close to thirty." She couldn't keep the note of pride from her voice. "Phillip finished law school last year and joined a firm in Knoxville. Cassie has a master's degree in computer programming and works for NASA in Huntsville. And there you have it: one woman's family."

"That's some family. Almost thirty people!" he exclaimed, giving a silent whistle as he slanted her a startled look. "You realize that the DeLords outnumber the Planchets almost two to one. Are you going to want all your sisters for bridesmaids?"

"Worrying about a circus wedding again?" she couldn't help teasing, tracing the pattern of his collarbone with the tip of her finger. As much as she loved them, she really didn't want to think about her family right now.

"Just wondering where we're going to put all of them if they all come to visit at one time. Maybe eloping wouldn't be such a bad idea, after all."

"You don't have to worry about being outnumbered. My family is very quiet in comparison to yours. Maybe we are more self-contained because there are so many of us," she said thoughtfully, thinking of the night of Tory's rehearsal dinner. "I don't think a wedding with our families and friends will need the riot police, unless your father gets out of hand. As long as you show up, I'll be happy."

"Will you be serious? We need to talk about our wedding."

"Will *I* be serious?" she echoed in amazement. "If I didn't know better, I'd think someone besides Trevor Planchet was in this bed with me. When did you turn into such a traditionalist?"

"From the moment I looked across the room and fell in love with a beautiful fairy-tale princess," he stated to her satisfaction, finally losing interest in her family. Trevor moved suddenly, shifting her onto her back to prove his statement with a persuasive kiss that ended much too soon. "I wake up every morning wondering if you're just a dream."

"We're in this dream together," she reassured him, linking her arms around his neck. "Are we through talking about my family now?"

"Mmmm," he answered against the vulnerable skin of her neck. "Right now I'm thinking about engagement rings."

"What?"

Propping himself up on his elbows, he gave her an earnest look. "I think it's past time I got a ring on your finger. There are a few former husband candidates out there who need to be warned off. You're mine now, Jessica DeLord, and I want the world to know it in no uncertain terms. How do you feel about diamonds?"

"Why don't you surprise me?" she said sweetly, gliding her hands down his rib cage. It was time for her to take control of this conversation. After children, her family, weddings, and engagement rings, she wasn't sure what he'd come up with, and she wasn't going to take any chances. She trailed her fingers over his hips, moving her hands between their warm bodies to show him exactly what was on her mind.

"Oh, Jessie," he managed hoarsely as she discovered that his thoughts weren't so far from her own.

"Why didn't you say you wanted to work on having a baby again?"

"Shut up and love me, Trevor," she murmured as she felt the full weight of his body against hers.

"For the rest of my life, sweetheart," he pledged, capturing her lips in a heated kiss of promise. "Don't ever forget how much I love you, Jessie."

Thursday morning, she ran the conversation over and over in her mind, trying to remember every word. It had been the last meaningful discussion she'd had with Trevor before he had disappeared the next morning. He'd been gone when she had waked. She hadn't heard a word in twenty-four hours, and she was beginning to worry.

The peal of the phone on her desk broke into her thoughts. "Hello. Timothy, you were supposed to be finished last week. I know your brother broke his arm, but I have to have wallpaper up by Saturday at four o'clock to be ready for the tour. Yes, please see if you can find someone to take his place."

"Something wrong?" Gina asked the moment Jessie slammed the receiver back down.

"What isn't? I'm not sure Trevor is going to have furniture on the first floor at the rate this is going. The first delivery was two days late, so who knows what will happen if the rest of it gets behind schedule."

"You still haven't heard from Trevor?" Gina asked as she handed her a cup of tea. "This should help your nerves."

"Nothing but that silly note telling me he would be out of town for a few days and to go ahead with finishing the house." Jessie exhaled heavily, not sure how to express her frustration at this point. "I can't get a straight answer from anyone. Even the tour committee is giving me fits; they've all suddenly become as vague as Mrs. Langford-Hughes. No one knows a thing about the refreshments and entertainment for the gazebo, not even the house chair. We have only two days left, and she said she would have to get back to me.''

''Don't start pulling your hair out yet. There's probably a very good explanation for all of this. You know that Quapaw tours are a great success every year, and have been for thirty years,'' Gina reasoned, slipping into the chair by Jessie's desk. ''You know how committee work is. The right hand doesn't know what the left is doing half the time. By Saturday this will all be a tempest in a teapot.''

''I don't care about the committee. I'm worried about Trevor,'' she muttered, swinging around to look at her quintet of rabbits lined up along the credenza. ''He hasn't even sent me a new bunny.''

''I'm not sure he could.''

''What do you mean?'' Jessie asked anxiously, knowing that she was acting like a fool.

''I think the bunny in the towel was risqué enough. He was that man who answered your phone Monday morning at eight o'clock, wasn't he?'' she asked dryly, giving her friend a speculative look. ''I got the shock of my life when I called to see why you were late for work, and Trevor answered the phone. You've been late for work three days this week. Exactly what kind of bunny were you expecting?''

''I don't know. I guess I'm just a little paranoid,'' Jessie admitted reluctantly. ''Everything has happened so fast. The man asked me to marry him, and now he's gone. If he shows up in one piece, I'm going to strangle him.''

''Yes, it certainly sounds like you're in love,'' Gina murmured and got up to return to her desk.

The next morning Jessie was ready to hire a hit man, not content to wait for Trevor to reappear in her life.

She entered the office after lunch with her temper boiling. There were still bedroom walls to be completed at the house. She would undoubtedly be up half the night supervising the wallpaper hanger and wondering where the second shipment of furniture from Dallas had gone. It wasn't in Little Rock, Arkansas.

"No. That's right. Okay, that will work. Uh-huh. Not right now." Gina waved as she continued her cryptic phone call. "That's not possible at the moment. I'll have to call you back."

"Any messages?" Jessie asked listlessly, knowing the answer before she heard it.

"Mr. Devon called about his wall hanging, and the Curley-Q Hair Saloon would like us to do an estimate. That's it."

"Do you think the library would let me have my baby and husband-hunting books back?" she asked idly while going through the mail. "I'll rip up the tax form for my donations if they do."

"Jessie, what's going through your mind?"

"Nothing really. It would just give me something to do while I'm waiting for the man to show up again," she grumbled, flopping down behind her desk. "Are you still coming to the house tomorrow night before the tour starts?"

"Actually, I don't think I can make it after all." Gina shuffled her feet and gave an apologetic shrug. "Jeff called a little while ago, and I think he's made plans for us. I'm sorry. I know you wanted me to be there—"

"Don't worry about it. It's not your fault—" Jessie broke off as she looked toward the entrance. T. L. Planchet was waving at her through the glass. A moment later, he stepped into the office, having to maneuver carefully because of the large box under his arm. "Good afternoon, ladies. Isn't it a glorious day out? I understand they're forecasting excellent weather for the tour tomorrow. How are things going?''

''Maybe you shouldn't ask, T.L.,'' Gina answered quickly.

''Not so good, I see.'' His brown eyes narrowed as he studied Jessie, waiting for her answer.

''No, we're running behind on everything. Tr-Trevor was right when he said the schedule was too tight,'' she informed him, attempting to keep her voice light. Then, unable to mask her curiosity over his appearance, she asked, ''What can we help you with today? That should cheer us up.''

''Oh, I think it will. If you would be so good as to close your eyes, Jessie.''

''Pardon?'' She wasn't quite sure she'd heard him correctly.

''Humor me and close your eyes,'' he said good-naturedly, giving her a broad wink, ''then I'll tell you my business.''

She obeyed his instructions, completely bewildered by this turn of events. At the sound of rustling tissue paper she cocked her head to the side, trying to figure out what was happening.

''All right, my dear. You can open your eyes now,'' he called out.

Jessie opened her eyes to find T.L. and Gina holding the most beautiful ivory lace dress she had ever seen. She couldn't resist stepping around her desk to touch the soft material. The design looked like something straight out of an old lithograph.

''This is your dress for tomorrow, I believe. I'm just the delivery boy.''

''Is Trevor back? Why hasn't he called me?'' she asked anxiously, trying not to let her old fears resurrect themselves. She'd held them at bay all week, only to be swamped by doubts at the most inappropriate times.

"No, he called last night to say he was delayed," T.L. replied, draping the dress over her arm. "He said he'd be back tomorrow and that you should wear this for the tour. That's all."

Unable to call Trevor a few harsh names in front of his father, Jessie laid the dress across her desk and began to pace the room. "T.L., does any of this make sense to you? I'm at my wits' end trying to get this house done on time, and he's disappeared into thin air for three days."

"I know it looks strange, but just be patient. I'm sure he'll be able to explain everything tomorrow," he said consolingly, his usual bluff manner not in evidence. "Why don't you plan to take a few days off next week? After a hectic week like this, I'm sure you could use the rest."

"That's not a bad idea, Jessie," Gina chimed in.

She looked back and forth between her partner and Trevor's father. Were they trying to tell her something, or was her imagination running off on a tangent? Right now she didn't have time to think. Even if Trevor had been in town, she still would have had to deal with paper hangers with broken arms, uncooperative committee members, and missing furniture.

Her only glimmer of hope was that Trevor would be here tomorrow and the tour would be history by Monday. If she could just hold on to her sanity that long, she was sure she could survive. She wasn't sure, however, how she would react if Trevor was still missing tomorrow.

Standing in the living room of the Dalrymple house at four-thirty on Saturday afternoon, Jessie wondered if she could slip out to the back garden and have a quiet nervous breakdown. The quiet chimes of the grandfather clock in the entry echoed through the house. Everything was done that could be done.

The last piece of wallpaper had been hung almost at the stroke of midnight. Jessie had crawled into Trevor's brass bed alone, hoping against hope that he would be beside her when she woke up. He hadn't been. She'd occupied her time removing drop cloths from the bedroom furniture, rehanging two sets of drapes, and waiting for the furniture delivery.

Wiping a weary hand across her forehead, she surveyed the room. The furniture had arrived two hours earlier, four hours late thanks to a flat tire. Looking around at the beautiful room, she felt the glow of pride begin to blossom inside her. By using traditional colors and plants, she'd created an illusion of the Victorian period without the clutter. The older pieces blended easily with the new.

Her sense of accomplishment was bittersweet because there was no one here to share it with her, at least not the person she wanted. Where was Trevor?

"Jessie, why aren't you dressed yet?" called Tory Herrington from behind her. Jessie whirled around to find Tory and Logan standing in the archway. Both of them were in formal attire, just as half the people on tonight's tour would be.

"What are you doing here?"

"We're here to help, but there isn't any time for questions," the brunette said sharply, giving her husband her purse and shawl. "The tour guides are scheduled to be here in less than an hour, so let's get shaking."

Jessie didn't put up any resistance when Tory took her hand and practically dragged her up the stairs. With a surprising talent for organization, Tory had Jessie in and out of the shower and standing in her floor-length slip in less than fifteen minutes. Jessie found herself plunked down at the vanity table in the dressing room off the master bedroom before she knew it. As Tory efficiently dealt with her hair and makeup, Jessie fancifully imagined she was a Victorian grande dame being prepared for some social event by her personal maid.

"Good heavens, what's that noise?" she asked, coming out of her trance at the sound of off-key music.

"I think that's the string quartet tuning up for the entertainment later. My people arrived with Logan and me to set up the refreshments."

"You're doing the refreshments?" Jessie parroted foolishly. Maybe she had had her nervous breakdown without realizing it.

"My father is the only one who can get away with hiring my competition," Tory stated heatedly. "My brother may act like an idiot occasionally, but he isn't stupid. He also has excellent taste in clothes. So let's get you into this gorgeous dress."

Standing in front of the cheval mirror a few minutes later, Jessie agreed that Trevor had amazing taste. She looked just like the Victorian lady she'd imagined a few minutes ago. The dress fit her perfectly—the lace collar emphasized her slender neck and the mutton-chop sleeves and wasp waist accentuated her willowy figure. It was as if the dress had been made for her.

"I knew you'd look exactly like that."

Jessie barely had time to glimpse Trevor's reflection in the mirror before he spun her around and crushed her in his arms. She flung her arms around his neck, relaying all her frustrations and anxieties into the embrace. The first touch of his lips breathed life back into her, making her feel alive for the first time in days. She forgot everything but the warm hands caressing her back and the hard, moist lips roaming over her face.

"It's about time you got here." Tory's accusation broke into Jessie's euphoria.

Trevor pressed Jessie's head against his shoulder and glared at his sister. "Don't you have to be someplace, Victoria?" His mellow voice rumbled under Jessie's ear at a counterpoint to his rapid heartbeat.

"I had to help Jessie get cleaned up for the guests, remember? You be nice to her. She deserves it after the past few days," his sister ordered, then stomped out of the room.

"That's exactly what I was going to say," Jessie mumbled against his ruffled shirt front before she raised her head, her smile softening the effect.

"Miss me?"

"Do I know you?" she asked innocently. "You look vaguely familiar, but I can't quite place where we've met before."

"I guess I deserved that," he admitted with a rueful smile, kissing her nose. "I thought I wouldn't be gone longer than a day and a half tops, and it kept dragging on and on. I never guessed that this would be the worst time for me to go out of town or that it would be so hellacious for you."

"It wouldn't have been so bad if you'd been here. Where were you?" Jessie pulled back to inspect the tuxedo he was wearing. He looked like he'd stepped off the pages of a glossy magazine. The tux was custom-made for his broad shoulders and narrow waist. He wore it with a negligence that said he was accustomed to formal dress.

"Hey, are you paying attention?" He tipped her chin up, stealing another kiss. "I have to stop that, or we'll get caught by the tourists. I went to Maryland to get something for you. This."

"This" was a yellow marquis diamond in an old-fashioned gold setting that he held between his finger and thumb. Jessie tried to swallow, but her mouth and throat had gone completely dry. She wasn't knowledgeable about gems, but she knew this one was spectacular. Her eyes misted over, and all she could manage was, "Oh, Trevor."

"That'll do." He gently pushed the ring on her finger and kissed it in place. "Does that mean you will marry me? None of this nonsense about a new relationship and taking time to get adjusted to each other?"

"Where did you get this ring?" she asked suspiciously, beginning to realize that there had been a plan behind his disappearance. She'd foolishly told him to surprise her without considering how Trevor didn't believe in half measures.

"It's my maternal grandmother's engagement ring," he said softly while brushing back a tendril of her hair from her temple. "All I planned to do was take a quick trip to Maryland and get the ring. Only Gran insisted she had to come back with me, and it took forever for her to rearrange her schedule. She insisted that she wanted to see her only grandson married as well as bringing the family veil."

"Trevor?" An apprehensive shiver went down her spine. Even he wouldn't do what she was thinking, she thought nervously, but then she spied for the first time the froth of antique lace lying on the bed.

"Yeah, this is going to be the hard part. Come on." He clutched her hand and barely gave her time to lift the hem of her skirt before he strode toward the hall. She realized that he was headed for the small balcony at the back of the house. Stepping out into the late-afternoon sunshine, Jessie was amazed to see what had taken place behind her back.

The gazebo was festooned with white ribbons and white baskets filled with spring flowers. More white ribbons and bows formed a walkway from the house to the gazebo with several rows of white folding chairs on either side. Catching a glimpse of her mother and Aunt

Lena talking to Gina, Jessie spun around to confront her fiancé.

"I thought you wanted to elope?" she accused him, stunned by what he had done. And she knew that he hadn't done it alone. This had all the earmarks of a major conspiracy.

"A man in love resorts to some desperate measures when he finally convinces his lady that he's the right man," he said solemnly, gathering her hands together in his. "I wanted to be sure you didn't start checking that list again and find someone who would make a better husband and father. It seemed so easy when I discovered there's no blood test or waiting period in Arkansas. T.L.'s clout helped with some minor details."

"I don't know whether to kiss you senseless or push you over the railing," she exclaimed, wondering if she should laugh or cry at his audacity.

"I vote for the kissing part," he stated firmly. "One thing I've learned this week is that I'll have to curb my impulses. Until now I haven't had to worry about any-one but myself. Loving someone makes you responsible to them."

How could he do this to her? she thought wildly, looking down at the people beginning to gather in the garden below them. He'd managed to get Betsy here from Missouri as well as her brother Miles all the way from South Dakota. Though she didn't see all of them, she was sure that almost thirty DeLord relatives were waiting below. What did a woman do with a man like this, a man who plans a beautiful wedding on the spur of the moment? How many men would dare such a thing? Only hers.

Looking up into his anxious brown eyes, Jessie knew exactly what she was going to do with a man who believed in spontaneity instead of organization and planning. "You realize that you're committing yourself to forty or fifty years of revenge for the last seventy-two hours you just put me through?''

"Oh, Jessie, I'm an idiot. I didn't even think about how you'd worry. Believe me, I'm never going to stay away from you more than twenty-four hours again,'' he murmured against her lips. The kiss was one to heal the hurt he had caused by his impetuous behavior. "I knew if I talked to you even once that I would blurt out all the plans. So put me out of my misery, please. Are you going to marry me?''

"Yes, sir,'' she said primly, just as her mother had trained her. They wouldn't have a placid marriage, she knew, but she didn't care. Both of them were willing to adjust to each other's idiosyncrasies. "I hope you know how lucky you are that I have a forgiving nature.''

"We're a lucky couple already with twelve rabbits' feet in the family,'' he answered proudly before guiding her back into the house.

"Twelve? I only have five rab— Trevor, what have you done?''

"You haven't seen the cake yet,'' he said impishly, which set Jessie off into a fit of giggles at the thought of a bunny bride and groom. She hoped they were scaled to the size of the cake. "I hear they're very fertile, you know.''

"Jessie, you can't stay in there and pout all night.'' Trevor's frustrated words were accompanied by a thump on the bathroom door.

Looking at her reflection in the gilt-framed mirror, Jessie decided she was just about ready to join her husband of eight hours in their honeymoon suite. Pouting was the last thing on her mind as she sprayed perfume in her cleavage, but Trevor didn't have to know that.

With one last look at her ice-blue satin gown, she opened the door.

The bedroom room of the bridal suite was dark; the only light was the moonlight coming through the open sliding-glass door to the balcony that overlooked the Arkansas River. She heard the clink of glasses and realized that her husband had taken the champagne onto the balcony.

"I wasn't pouting, but I do think you could have told me you were younger than I—" She broke off as she crossed the threshold and caught a glimpse of her bridegroom silhouetted by the full moon overhead. Laughter burst from her lips, making her clutch the curtain to keep her balance.

"I was trying to be romantic and remind you of our first meeting," he said with mock dignity, straightening his rabbit ears. He stood by the railing, loose-fitting white pants riding low on his lean hips. The white vest was missing from his ensemble, but Jessie didn't mind.

"What else could I expect from a younger man?" Jessie finally managed, walking toward him in slow, measured steps. "Maybe I should have worn my red satin outfit, since you're being nostalgic."

"Not nostalgic, just testing you to see if it's really me you fell in love with or my manly chest."

"Your manly chest, of course." Jessie proved her statement by sliding her hands over his warm skin to entwine her arms around his neck. "I think I'm going to toss those ears of yours in the river so you won't proposition any other unsuspecting women."

"Only if they look like a fairy-tale princess, have legs that go on forever, and are named Jessica," he murmured while nibbling kisses along her jawline. "Did you have to wear a long nightgown?"

"I thought you'd like the challenge," she whispered in return, beginning an exploration of her own. "I'm a little new at the seduction game, but I think I did better with my selection than yours.''

"I think we tied. Each of us wants to take off what the other is wearing.'' He proved his point by slipping the strap of her gown off her shoulder and branding her skin with a fervent kiss.

Jessie reached up for his ears, plucked them from his head, but didn't throw them into the river. Instead, she held them against her cheek for a moment. "I'm relieved to see these little darlings. You were almost too serious most of the evening, even when the news crew showed up to cover the wedding. You didn't even yell at T.L. for arranging that. I was beginning to think I'd married a stranger—a *young* stranger.''

"Does it really bother you that I'm almost four years younger than you?'' He raised his head to look deep into her eyes.

"Not now, but a few weeks ago I might have used it against you. Just one more thing I would have used to defend myself,'' she admitted with a rueful smile, "before I surrendered to the inevitable. I kept telling myself you weren't the responsible, sensible man I needed in my life.''

"I'm surprised my behavior this week didn't cinch it,'' he muttered, running his fingers through her loose hair. "My big romantic gesture turned into a lot of work and frustration for you while I was trotting off to Maryland.''

"Trevor, one thing I've learned since I met you is that I need romantic gestures in my life.'' Jessie cupped his face in her hands, standing on tiptoe to kiss the crook in his nose. "Look what being too serious did for me—got me a date with someone like Connor MacMurray. Can you imagine what kind of husband and father he would make, if some woman was crazy enough to marry him? He probably makes love on a schedule and wouldn't ever think of sending anyone a stuffed rabbit.''

"Speaking of rabbits and children, why don't we go test that theory about women reaching their sexual peak in their late thirties?'' He picked her up before she could say a word, but she reached down and snagged the champagne bucket as they passed the table.

"I promise never to bring up your age again if you stop making rabbit jokes,'' Jessie declared solemnly, softening her words by feathering a kiss along his cheek.

"Does this mean you don't want any more bunnies, even on our anniversaries?'' Trevor asked as he sat down on the bed, Jessie held snugly on his lap. "And aren't bunnies supposed to be ideal for decorating nurseries?''

"I told you that we don't have to start a family immediately,'' she informed him as he took the silver bucket from her and placed it on the nightstand. Snuggling into the cradle of his shoulder, she chastised him. "You even told my mother the bunnies on the wedding cake were a traditional fertility symbol in your family.''

"That's because she and Lena were telling T.L. how disappointed they both were that they didn't have more grandchildren,'' he returned absently, his lips exploring the nape of her neck. "I wanted to make a good impression on my new mothers-in-law.''

"You're making a very good impression on their daughter right now, Mr. Planchet,'' she almost sighed as his hand closed over her breast.

"That's all I've ever wanted to do from the very beginning, Jessie love.'' He placed her across the satin bedspread, hovering over her. When she reached up to entwine her arms around his neck, he forestalled her. "I promise you, Jessica Planchet, that from now on all the misadventures are behind us. You'll never be sorry that you trusted me with your love. You've gotten yourself that dependable, responsible husband after all."

Jessie didn't bother to answer in words, simply smiling as she pulled his head down until his mouth covered hers. As she lost herself in Trevor's embrace, she knew that she was in for the adventure of her life, her own personal wonderland with an incredibly sexy white rabbit as her personal guide.

EPILOGUE

"Which one do you think will give in first?" Tory Herrington asked her sister-in-law as they sat on the porch swing of T.L.'s house watching the men and children play.

"Never-Say-Die Planchet give in to No-Guts-No-Glory Herrington? It's a tough choice," Jessie answered, taking a long sip on her lemonade. She winced as Trevor went sprawling on the soft grass of his father's side lawn. "I thought soccer wasn't a contact sport."

"It isn't supposed to be. Those two clowns made up their own game of tackle-soccer. These days I'm not sure who's more immature, my brother or my husband. I think I've taught Logan to be a little too laid back."

"If Trevor thinks I'm letting my son play this stupid game, he's crazy," Jessie muttered, looking across the lawn for the black-haired urchin in question. She spotted the four-year-old sitting in the gazebo with his three-year-old cousin, Miriam Herrington, listening to Arnette read Dr. Seuss.

"I don't think you have to worry about Chase, but you'd better watch out for Darcy." Tory pointed to the three-year-old girl running like her father's shadow along the sidelines.

"Tell me something I don't know. She's given both Trevor and me a few more gray hairs than we need," she informed her quickly. "This morning he found her trying to learn how to fly by jumping off the balcony. She told us, and I quote, 'I don't need a parachute because my wings are dynamically sound.' "

"Hey, darlin', have you got a kiss for a needy man?" Trevor easily scaled the porch railing and stole his kiss before he got an answer.

"A hot and sweaty man," Jessie declared, wrinkling her nose as she smiled up at him. A movement behind her grinning husband quickly distracted her. "Okay, hotshot, turn around and grab your daughter. She's following your example of avoiding the steps."

"Whoops." With practiced reflexes, he swiftly scooped up Darcy, then perched on the railing with his daughter sitting snugly in his lap. "So what horrible plot are you two hatching?"

"Well, I was just about to ask your sister what we should do for your fortieth birthday," Jessie explained sweetly. "Or would you like us to ask your Daddy to plan it?"

"You still haven't forgiven me for that, have you?"

"For what?" Logan asked as he came around the corner with two beers in his hand.

"My sneaky husband tricked me into marrying him by withholding vital information." Jessie gave Trevor a look that dared him to contradict her. His salacious grin in answer sent a shiver of delight skating up her spine.

"It wasn't that important," he responded before taking a swig from the water-beaded can in his hand.

"I didn't realize it was going to be then," she shot back, her eyes gleaming with amusement, answering the promise of his smile with one of her own. Even a mock argument deserved a passionate reconciliation, and her husband always enjoyed proving his point about the sensuality of older woman. "I heard you tell Chase that you were going to be as old as Mama pretty soon. He asked me if I as as old as Granner this morning."

"And a fine-looking woman she is," Trevor responded hardily, gesturing for the others to join in a toast to the lady. "Now admit you married me because I'm a sexy devil."

"Daddy's a silly devil," Darcy chanted and wiggled to get down, skipping off to join her older brother in the gazebo.

"I think I need to have a talk with my daughter." Trevor looked thoughtfully after the little girl before casting a suspicious eye at his sister. "You haven't been coaching her, have you?"

"Be nice, or I won't babysit for your kids next weekend," she shot back.

"What's this?" His dark eyes took on a speculative gleam as he turned to look at his wife, who was squirming in her seat.

"Why is it, no matter what, I can never surprise the man? He managed to spring an entire wedding on me, but I still haven't managed one tiny little surprise," Jessie complained good-naturedly as Tory apologized for her blunder.

"It takes time to learn to be conniving and crafty like the Planchets," Logan stated firmly in her defense. "You and I have been exposed to the breed for only a short period of time."

"Very true." She nodded in agreement, waiting for the expected protests from Tory and Trevor.

"I'll have you know you stunned me when you told me you were pregnant with Darcy," her husband related with a grin. "We hadn't planned on that little dividend. I guess all those rabbits did the trick after all.''

''I guess I deserved that one,'' Jessie admitted, but didn't hesitate to throw an ice cube at her unrepentant husband. He dodged easily out of the way. ''I did promise not to tease you about your age if you'd give up rabbit jokes.''

The cry of a baby from inside the house kept Trevor from answering immediately.

''That sounds like little Preston.'' Tory got to her feet as she spoke. Linking her arm with her husband, she asked, ''Want to come help me feed your son?''

''Don't mind if I do,'' he answered quickly, an amorous smile curving his lips.

As the couple disappeared around the corner of the porch, Trevor slipped into his sister's place on the swing. Dropping an arm around his wife's shoulders, he pulled her close to his side, his fingers toying with the strap of her sundress. ''Too bad we don't have the excuse of feeding the baby to slip away.''

''Too true, but somebody's got to watch the kids until Curtiss and Leeanne get here,'' Jessie answered, turning her face up for his kiss.

''That's the one thing they didn't put in the baby books—the lack of privacy for the more important things in life,'' he stated hoarsely as his lips claimed hers.

''Daddy's a silly devil,'' exclaimed a high-pitched voice from directly in front of them.

''Didn't Gina say she and Jeff wanted a little girl?'' Trevor asked as he reached out to tickle his daughter, a carbon copy of himself.

Jessie's laughter blended with Darcy's giggles. ''She was talking about having a little sister for David. Besides she turned you down the last time you offered to sell her the kids, the day that Darcy put epoxy in your running shoes, I think.''

"So where are we running away to for my birthday?'' he asked after he sent his daughter into the kitchen, where Arnette had taken Miriam and Chase for cookies.

"Damn, I thought you might have forgotten about that.''

"Not if it involves spending time alone with my incredibly sexy wife,'' he murmured, returning his attention to the hollow of her neck. "I love my kids, but I have this incredible thing for their mother. I don't get to have her all to myself very often, and I cherish the moments.''

"Oh, so do I,'' Jessie murmured, covering his lips with her own. After almost five years of marriage, she was more in love with Trevor than the day she had married him. The adventure had lasted and only improved with age. Her impulsive, outrageous husband made each day special, and she wouldn't change a thing about him.

SHARE THE FUN . . .
SHARE YOUR NEW-FOUND TREASURE!!

You don't want to let your new books out of your sight?
That's okay. Your friends can get their own. Order below.

No. 3 SOUTHERN HOSPITALITY by Sally Falcon
North meets South. War is declared. Both sides win!!!

No. 30 REMEMBER THE NIGHT by Sally Falcon
Joanna throws caution to the wind. Is Nathan fantasy or reality?

No. 55 A FOREVER MAN by Sally Falcon
Max is trouble and Sandi wants no part of him. She *must* resist!

No. 107 STOLEN KISSES by Sally Falcon
In Jessie's search for Mr. Right, Trevor was definitely a wrong turn!

No. 68 PROMISE OF PARADISE by Karen Lawton Barrett
Gabriel is surprised to find that Eden's beauty is not just skin deep.

No. 69 OCEAN OF DREAMS by Patricia Hagan
Is Jenny just another shipboard romance to Officer Kirk Moen?

No. 70 SUNDAY KIND OF LOVE by Lois Faye Dyer
Trace literally sweeps beautiful, ebony-haired Lily off her feet.

No. 71 ISLAND SECRETS by Darcy Rice
Chad has the power to take away Tucker's hard-earned independence.

No. 72 COMING HOME by Janis Reams Hudson
Clint always loved Lacey. Now Fate has given them another chance.

No. 73 KING'S RANSOM by Sharon Sala
Jesse was always like King's little sister. When did it all change?

No. 74 A MAN WORTH LOVING by Karen Rose Smith
Nate's middle name is 'freedom' . . . that is, until Shara comes along.

No. 75 RAINBOWS & LOVE SONGS by Catherine Sellers
Dan has more than one problem. One of them is named Kacy!

No. 76 ALWAYS ANNIE by Patty Copeland
Annie is down-to-earth and real . . . and Ted's never met anyone like her.

No. 77 FLIGHT OF THE SWAN by Lacey Dancer
Rich had decided to swear off romance for good until Christiana.

No. 78 TO LOVE A COWBOY by Laura Phillips
Dee is the dark-haired beauty that sends Nick reeling back to the past.

No. 79 SASSY LADY by Becky Barker
No matter how hard he tries, Curt can't seem to get away from Maggie.

No. 80 CRITIC'S CHOICE by Kathleen Yapp
Marlis can't do one thing right in front of her handsome houseguest.

No. 81 TUNE IN TOMORROW by Laura Michaels
Deke happily gave up life in the fast lane. Can Liz do the same?

No. 82 CALL BACK OUR YESTERDAYS by Phyllis Houseman
Michael comes to terms with his past with Laura by his side.

No. 83 ECHOES by Nancy Morse
Cathy comes home and finds love even better the second time around.

No. 84 FAIR WINDS by Helen Carras
Fate blows Eve into Vic's life and he finds he can't let her go.

No. 85 ONE SNOWY NIGHT by Ellen Moore
Randy catches Scarlett fever and he finds there's no cure.

No. 86 MAVERICK'S LADY by Linda Jenkins
Bentley considered herself worldly but she was not prepared for Reid.

No. 87 ALL THROUGH THE HOUSE by Janice Bartlett
Abigail is just doing her job but Nate blocks her every move.

Meteor Publishing Corporation
Dept. 992, P. O. Box 41820, Philadelphia, PA 19101-9828

Please send the books I've indicated below. Check or money order (U.S. Dollars only)—no cash, stamps or C.O.D.s (PA residents, add 6% sales tax). I am enclosing $2.95 plus 75¢ handling fee for *each* book ordered.

Total Amount Enclosed: $_____.

___ No. 3	___ No. 70	___ No. 76	___ No. 82
___ No. 30	___ No. 71	___ No. 77	___ No. 83
___ No. 55	___ No. 72	___ No. 78	___ No. 84
___ No. 107	___ No. 73	___ No. 79	___ No. 85
___ No. 68	___ No. 74	___ No. 80	___ No. 86
___ No. 69	___ No. 75	___ No. 81	___ No. 87

Please Print:
Name _____

Address _____ Apt. No. _____

City/State _____ Zip _____

Allow four to six weeks for delivery. Quantities limited.